"I want Darcy to be my new mom,"
Ricky said.

Joe looked at his son and felt a lump lodge in his throat. He'd hoped that Ricky had gotten over this desperation for a mother. But somehow the boy had decided that Darcy Beckett was the perfect maternal candidate.

Joe took a deep breath. Was there anything Darcy was *less* suited for? "Darcy is not the mom type," he said, more to himself than to Ricky.

"Why not?"

"Well, we like milkshakes. Darcy likes champagne. And every mouthful costs about as much as a box of crayons."

"Oh."

There was a long silence, and Joe thought, gratefully, that the subject was closed. Someday, he told himself, his son would understand. And when he did, maybe he could explain it to Joe.

"But what if she drank something else?" Ricky piped up. *"Then* could she be my new mom?"

TRUE LOVE RANCH

Elizabeth Harbison

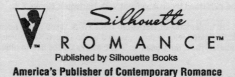

Silhouette

ROMANCE™

Published by Silhouette Books

America's Publisher of Contemporary Romance

To Annie Jones and Natalie Patrick
both excellent writers...and one heck of a great friend.

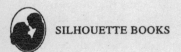 SILHOUETTE BOOKS

ISBN 0-373-19323-8

TRUE LOVE RANCH

Printed in U.S.A.

Books by Elizabeth Harbison

Silhouette Romance

A Groom for Maggie #1239
Wife Without a Past #1258
Two Brothers and a Bride #1286
True Love Ranch #1323

ELIZABETH HARBISON

first thought of becoming a writer in sixth grade, when she would stay up well past midnight reading Nancy Drew and Trixie Beldon books under the covers by flashlight. The idea became a decision when she discovered the books of Mary Stewart and Dorothy Eden, and realized that writing would be a really *fun* thing to do for a living.

She studied literature and art history at the University of Maryland and the University of London, Birbeck College. She's been back to England once since college and is eager to return again, and possibly even set a book there.

The author of several cookbooks, Elizabeth spends her spare time cooking, reading, walking and shopping for new books. As for romance, her fairy-tale dreams came true in 1994 when she married her real-life hero, John, a musician and illustrator. They currently reside in Germantown, Maryland, with their daughter, Mary Paige, and dog, Bailey.

Elizabeth loves to hear from her readers. You can write to her at P.O. Box 1636, Germantown, MD 20875-1636.

October 7, 1997

Ms. Darcy Beckett
3631 Dasher Street #4
Boston, MA

Dear Ms. Beckett,

As you are no doubt aware, R. Kenneth Beckett passed away on October 6 of this year.

You are a beneficiary in his will, which will be read on Friday, October 22, at noon. This meeting will take place on Mr. Beckett's property, known as the "True Love Ranch," in Holt, Colorado. If at all possible, please come to that reading…but beware—the True Love Ranch is thought to have magical powers for reuniting former lovers….

I look forward to meeting you.

Sincerely,

Edward J. Connor, Esq.
Attorney for Mr. R. Kenneth Beckett

*Cindy, please make a duplicate letter and send it to
Mr. Joseph Tyler
R.R. 8, Box 92
Holt, CO

Thanks,
Edward

Prologue

"Darcy, honey, can you finish making the pies? If I don't get out and help the men set up outside this is going to be the most sparse Fourth of July party ever."

Anthea Cox had worked as the housekeeper and general caretaker on Darcy's grandfather's ranch for as long as she could remember.

"Sure, Anthea." Darcy Beckett looked out the window. Eight hired hands, her grandfather and Anthea's husband, Hank, were milling about rather aimlessly. "You tell them, Anthea. We women shouldn't have to do *all* the work."

Anthea put her arm around Darcy's shoulder and gave her a warm hug. "That's right, child. You remember that. Men and women should *share* responsibilities in this life, as well as pleasures."

Darcy flushed at her private thought of pleasure and took another look outside. Where was Joe? The youngest—and strongest, Darcy thought proudly—of Kenneth Beckett's hired hands, Joe Tyler was always roped into tasks like this. She'd seen him there a few minutes ago.

"Looking for someone?" Anthea asked over her shoulder.

"I'm just looking out the window." Darcy's skin tingled with anticipation.

Anthea gave her a knowing look. "Don't see that Tyler boy out there." She clicked her tongue against her teeth. "Pity. You'd have such a fine view from here."

Darcy's face grew hot, but she laughed. "You always could see right through me."

Anthea went to the refrigerator and took out a chilled lump of pastry dough for the pies. "Just see to it that your grandfather doesn't see through you that way."

"He doesn't understand anything about love," Darcy said miserably. She knew if her grandfather found out about her and Joe, the consequences would be dire.

"He knows a thing or two, but he can be a little too…vehement. At times."

"Mean is more the word."

"He's just looking out for you." Anthea put a sympathetic hand on Darcy's shoulder. "He doesn't want you to get hurt."

"I'm old enough to take care of myself."

Anthea smiled. "At your age, I thought I knew all about love, too. I didn't."

There was a whoop of laughter from the men outside and Anthea flashed an impatient look in that direction. "I'd better get out there. Folks'll be coming in an hour."

Darcy took the chilled dough and began pressing it down with the heel of her hand. "I'll take care of this, don't worry."

Anthea bustled out the kitchen door. As soon as she was gone, Darcy sighed and allowed herself a moment's indulgence in thinking about Joe. Last night had been magical. Better than she'd ever imagined it could be.... She shivered with remembered pleasure. She knew about love, all right.

She picked up the apron and moved back to the window. Where *was* Joe anyway? Just as she was reaching behind her to tie the straps, she felt hands on hers. "Need some help, ma'am?" Joe asked, close to her ear.

She whirled to face him. "We shouldn't be in here alone together, you know."

He reached behind her to tie the straps. "I'm only helping a lady in distress." He stopped tying and rested his hands on her lower back.

"Is that all you're doing?" she teased.

"That and kissing my future wife." He lowered his mouth onto hers and kissed her. Darcy's passions flared, quickly reaching a state close to what she'd felt last night.

She pulled back, breathless. "W-wife?"

"Sure. You knew I'd make an honest woman of you, didn't you?"

She swallowed. "When?"

"How long before you're eighteen?" He gave a devilish smile. He knew darn well her birthday was in September— it was the day after his.

Her heart thundered in her ears. "Do you mean it?"

"More than anything." He kissed her again. "What do you say? Will you marry me?"

"Joe—"

"Say yes or I'll die."

She smiled. "Well..."

"Darce, I love you more than I've ever loved anyone in my life." His eyes burned with sincerity. "Do you love me?"

She looked down. *He loved her!* Her knees began to

shake. "Yes," she said, looking back at him. "I love you."

Something crossed his expression then: a boyish relief mingled with joy. "Then say yes."

"Yes."

He cupped her face in his hands and kissed her again, deeply. "How about we get ourselves a place just like this?"

"Like the ranch?"

"Like all of this." He swept his arm across the room. "You look good in this kitchen. I can see you here, making breakfast for me and the kids—"

Her heart skipped a beat. "Kids?"

He nodded. "Two or three of them. That okay with you?"

"I always wanted two kids," she said wistfully. "A boy and a girl."

He tipped an imaginary hat. "I'll do my best to help you out with that dream, ma'am."

She gave a tremulous smile. "If last night is an example of your help, I'll look forward to it."

"Last night was just the tip of the iceberg," he murmured and lowered his mouth onto hers again.

Her body flamed to life. She wrapped her arms around him and pressed her body along the length of his. She felt so safe in his embrace, so warm, so happy.

"What the hell is going on here?" a voice boomed from the doorway.

Darcy sprang back and looked, with horror, at the source of the angry demand.

It was her grandfather.

Chapter One

"**C**ome on, get out of the way!" Darcy glanced at her watch, then leaned on the horn of her dilapidated luxury car for the second time. "Let's get *moving* here."

Ahead of her, the brake lights on the pale blue pickup flared red, and the vehicle stopped. Stopped? That wasn't the response she'd been after.

Inside the truck, the driver moved as though to get out.

Darcy's breath caught in her throat. Boy she may have just aggravated the wrong guy. She looked around. The rough road that led to T.L. Ranch had barely enough room for one car and certainly no room for her to go around him. And she couldn't back up. The reverse gear had broken a week ago, and she'd been using the Fred Flintstone method ever since. She wasn't about to open the door now....

The driver's door of the pickup opened.

Darcy straightened her back and carefully reached for her purse on the seat next to her. Coming from Chicago, she knew not to take any chances with angry strangers. She had a stun gun and pepper spray at the ready at all times. Which should it be?

A booted leg extended out of the truck. And it was a big boot.

Pepper spray, Darcy decided.

She watched with bated breath as the driver unfolded himself from the truck. He straightened up to nearly seven feet tall, or so it seemed to her.

His hair was as black as licorice under a battered Stetson, and longish at the collar. His pale eyes narrowed when they touched upon her. If he weren't coming at her in that sinister way, she might have thought he was attractive—in a rustic sort of way. Faded denims, a Levi's shirt and scuffed leather boots completed the intimidating picture. He looked like an angry Paul Bunyan.

He walked slowly and steadily toward her. He wasn't as tall as she'd originally guessed; he was probably just over six feet, but his commanding air made him *seem* taller.

As he got closer, she realized he looked vaguely familiar. But how could that be? She hadn't been to her grandfather's ranch for ten years—since she was seventeen years old, and back then... Her heart pounded with a mixture of dread and excitement. Could it *possibly* be him?

No, surely he had left when she did.

Darcy glanced at the half-open window and pressed on the broken automatic-close button, knowing that it hadn't worked for a month. The cold November wind whipping around the inside of the car was a testament to that. But paying to have it fixed had fallen somewhere after eating on her hierarchy of needs.

She closed her eyes and said a silent prayer.

"You need something?" a deep voice asked.

She opened one eye and looked into the face of the truck driver. Her chest constricted. It looked like him, that was for sure. But it was just too far-fetched. He was long gone. "I beg your pardon?"

"I'm trying to figure out what it is you need." One side of his mouth twitched toward a smile but didn't quite make it. The brim of his hat was low over his brow, shading his features.

"What I *need?*" she repeated dumbly.

He pushed the rim of his hat up and she went still with shock. It *had* to be him. There couldn't be another man in the world who looked so like him. Faint laugh lines around his eyes made him a little less familiar than he would have been with the boyishly smooth skin she remembered. But it was him; she knew it.

"I heard your horn." His voice was lower, a little huskier than she expected. "Thought you might be signaling some distress." His mouth twitched into a half smile now. "Especially when it kept happening." He hesitated and scrutinized her. "Is everything all right?" he asked when she didn't respond.

"I'm— It's fine," she said, feeling her face warm.

"Wait just a minute." He leaned closer and her heart skipped a beat. "Are you who I think you are?"

It was him. Joe Tyler.

"I'm not sure…" she said vaguely, her heart pounding a furious beat that he could probably hear from a distance of three feet. "You are…?"

Of course she already knew the answer. He was Joseph Emory Tyler, though he hated his middle name. Favorite color: blue. Favorite dessert: chocolate pudding. Favorite rock group: the Beatles. Favorite sport: steer wrestling at the rodeo. They'd spent many long ago hours arguing over whether or not it was a humane sport. He'd wanted to be famous for it one day. In the meantime he was going to try to finish his college education in order to have something "to fall back on if the rodeo thing doesn't work out." He hated spinach, but ate it because he'd bought into the whole Popeye myth years before. He loved beef but hated pork—except sausages and bacon.

A long time ago, Darcy had adored him enough to…well, that didn't matter now. Maybe it had never mattered. It certainly hadn't mattered to him—that was clear then and it was just as clear now. Maybe more, since he was still here.

She swallowed her bitterness. That was history now. Her anger could only hurt her. She took a long breath, inwardly counting to five. She knew her face was a self-conscious blotchy red.

"Darcy Beckett?" he said, solidly confirming his recollection. "Little Darcy Beckett?"

She gave a shuddering sigh. Hearing him say her name did nothing to still her reaction. And he remembered the moniker that had made her so impatient back then. All of her grandfather's friends and employees, who'd known her since she was a baby, called her Little Darcy Beckett, but only Joe had done it in a low, teasing way. Then and now.

"Joe Tyler, right?" She hoped she sounded nonchalant.

He touched the brim of his hat and nodded. "How the hell have you been?"

"Fine," she said, a little too curtly. She thought of all the ways in which life had not been fine, but forced a smile. "How about you?" What in the world are you still doing here? she demanded silently.

"Just great." He shook his head again and gave a low

whistle. "I almost didn't recognize you, Darcy. Welcome back to the T.L. Ranch." Was it her imagination or was his voice tinged with irony?

Anyway, just who did he think he was, welcoming her back to her own grandfather's ranch? It was the closest thing she'd ever had to a real home, and yet she'd been sent away from it because of Joe Tyler. Now, here he was, welcoming her back in that lord-of-the-manner way of his. "It's good to finally be back," she said, hoping he noticed the chill in her tone.

Clearly unaware of the feelings churning inside her, Joe continued, "I guess you're here because of the will."

"That's right."

"Me, too."

Her heart pounded. "You?"

He nodded.

"Why?" Her voice sounded sharp, even to her own ears.

"I got a letter from the lawyer telling me to be there at four o'clock." He raised an eyebrow. "Of course, I'm usually there anyway—"

"Don't tell me you still work at the ranch." She tried to sound casual, as if she weren't grinding it out from between her teeth. Which she was.

"I do. Been there for twelve years now." He paused, and she wondered how much he knew about her estrangement from her grandfather. "I'm surprised your grandfather never mentioned it."

Shame burned in her cheeks. "We...didn't talk much in the last few years." Did he really not know that? Or was he baiting her, trying to get her to admit she'd lost touch?

Joe frowned, then his expression cleared. "That's

right.'' He snapped his fingers. "Now I remember the story. You ran off and married that guy no one liked. Whole family was mad at you.''

It was an accurate description, except he didn't mention the divorce. She gave a noncommittal nod.

Joe clicked his tongue against his teeth. "You and Ken stopped speaking all those years because of *that*?''

"It seemed best at the time." She didn't add that she'd tried to telephone Kenneth Beckett about fifty times in those first couple of years, but that he'd never taken her calls. She also didn't add that her Christmas cards had come back unopened. She couldn't bear to admit she hadn't even known her grandfather was ill, and she also didn't add that she'd hesitated even to come to the reading of the will for fear he'd left her a bag of coal as his final I-told-you-so.

Joe raised an eyebrow. "So where's your husband now?''

"My ex-husband, you mean.''

She could have sworn a look of mild surprise came into his eyes.

"The divorce just recently became final." Though she had known Brandon wasn't Prince Charming when she had married him, she had hoped that fact would protect her. If she didn't love him, how could he hurt her? She now knew how foolish that idea was. "And as for where he is, I don't know." Though she wished she did. Or, more specifically, she wished she knew where her money—which he had helped himself to upon his exit—was.

Joe regarded her for a moment, then with a very small inclination of the head, he said, "I'm sorry to hear it.''

She shrugged. "It's almost time for the meeting." She gestured at her watch. "We don't want to be late.''

"Right. Sure." After one final moment's perusal, he turned and headed back toward the truck. Darcy wondered if he could be completely unaware of how attractive he was viewed from the back, in his faded jeans and scuffed boots. Her heart flipped stupidly, just as it had so many times that summer when she was seventeen. The cool breeze lifted, carrying the familiar scent of the woods— like a ghost from her memory.

Darcy watched Joe for a moment, feeling a deep purple melancholy settle over her like a cloud. Tears pricked at her eyes and she blinked them away. Then she picked up the carefully folded lawyer's letter that was on the seat next to her and tried to concentrate. As if anything would stop the memories and the longing now that she was going to have to see Joe again. She unfolded the letter and glanced at the hand-drawn map on the back. She should remember the way, but it had been so long.

She could follow Joe, but pride compelled her to find the way for herself. She continued to look at the map. There was a broken-down shack somewhere up here on the right, but she couldn't recall such a thing. It was just one more reminder of how long it had been since she'd been at the ranch.

She looked back at the blue pickup, which had resumed its pitiful gait. It was deliberate, she knew. Joe hadn't changed much at all, now that she thought about it. He'd always been able to goad her more effectively than anyone.

The trick was to ignore him.

She thought about the ranch and wondered what would become of it. The lawyer's letter certainly made it sound as though it was her inheritance, but she couldn't believe that, given her grandfather's attitude toward her. She sighed. At least the letter said she could stay on for a while. That would give her a few days to regroup and plan the rest of her trip to California. Maybe she could even find a mechanic who would give her car the once-over without charging too much.

But then she'd be moving on. She'd spent too long in Chicago as it was—nearly five years. It was the longest Darcy had ever spent in one city. After the divorce, her friend Melanie, in San Diego, had said Darcy could share her place until she got on her feet. It wasn't the ideal situation, but Darcy was running out of options.

She'd spend a few days here—maybe a week—then move on. Forever. This wasn't home. That was just an illusion she'd created because it was out of her grasp. As long as the T.L. Ranch remained the single great bastion of home and safety in her mind, she would never be able to move forward. Once she'd spent a little time here, worked out some of her inner demons, she would be free of Colorado, the ranch, and memories of that summer with Joe Tyler…forever.

Then she'd be free to work on the Menger's grant scholarship program in San Diego. Louis Menger had been trying to get her on the project, which provided scholarships for inner-city teenagers, for three years. He was getting older now, and Darcy feared the scholarship program might falter if Louis stopped heading it and left the reins to someone else. It had been her father's pet project before he died, and Louis had long wanted Darcy to take it over.

The idea had always appealed to her, too. But her husband hadn't had much respect for any kind of nonprofit organization so she put it off. Now it sounded like the perfect project to sink her energies into. Darcy liked the idea of being responsible for helping to educate bright, worthy kids who might otherwise get lost in the system.

She wanted to make a *difference* in people's lives.

But she was going to do it by herself. Louis Menger might be offering her a job, but she was going to have to start her life on her own, without help. She was going to make a home for herself, *without* a man.

And she wouldn't let Joe Tyler—or her former, perhaps unresolved, feelings for him—get in the way.

She took a deep breath and felt the energy of possibility surge through her. For the first time in years she felt as though things really were going to work out for her. She had a purpose, a goal—and she was heading for it full speed.

There was only one thing standing between her and her dream.

Darcy looked at the truck in front of her and sighed heavily. She'd spent a lot of money on therapy trying to work out those lingering feelings for Joe. And she'd succeeded, she reminded herself. Years ago. Now he was a temporary obstacle. Not even an obstacle—just a distraction, that was all.

She had to remember that.

Joe looked in his rearview mirror at Darcy in her car. He sure hadn't thought he'd see her today, or any other time, come to think of it. Sure, she was getting the ranch and whatever other assets Ken had to be distributed, but from what Joe understood, Darcy was busy living the high life in Chicago. For her, this would be just one more asset to liquidate. At the most he would have expected her to send a representative. Joe felt he could have dealt with a representative. He wasn't so sure about Darcy. Somehow he was going to have to try not to let her get to him.

He'd just concentrate on his other business. There certainly was enough of it to keep him occupied. He pressed harder on the accelerator and the truck lurched forward.

Of course, the news of her divorce was a surprise. Maybe that was it—maybe she just wanted a change of scenery, something to help her forget the heartbreak.

Joe could have told her *some* things just can't be forgotten. Or ignored.

Her car drew up a little too close to his back bumper, and he found himself smiling. Typical Darcy, he thought, always in a hurry. Somehow, that bulldozer quality had always endeared her to him.

Watching her in his rearview mirror, he studied her, marveling at her beauty. The finely arched eyebrows, determined chin, curved mouth. He looked back at the road, but her image stayed with him. Dark blond hair, evenly cut at the shoulder. If the stories that had circulated about her at the ranch were true, she'd probably paid a fortune for that haircut back in Chicago.

She sure had changed since he'd known her. Way back then, money hadn't mattered to her one whit. At first he hadn't believed the stories about her lifestyle after she'd left the ranch, but eventually he'd admitted to himself that he hadn't *wanted* to believe them. The stories just made him feel that much more foolish for ever thinking they could make a go of it together.

Darcy Beckett, his wife, sharing ranch life with him—that had just been a stupid, immature dream.

He'd woken up a long time ago.

He looked back at her. Fancy car, fancy haircut. According to her grandfather, Darcy lived high off the hog. Drank champagne as though it were water. She probably even rinsed her mouth with it when she brushed her teeth. Or used fancy bottled water from France.

He glanced at the road to keep on course, then back at the mirror. Darcy was framed in its confines like a picture. For a moment, he saw her as she used to be. Her hair, which had been much lighter then, was long and straight. She used to live in jeans and T-shirts, not the kind of fancy clothes she was wearing now.

She'd grown up, and done a damn good job of it. He'd grant her that.

Her face...how many times had he seen that face in his dreams? She'd barely changed, he'd realized when he'd gotten up close. For a moment he'd gone dumb at the sight of those strong cheekbones and the stubborn chin he used to love to kiss. Her skin was as smooth-looking as ever. In memory, he could just reach out and touch her. In memory.

Hell, it wasn't easy to forget Darcy Beckett.

She used to come to the ranch every summer, though he hadn't met her until she was fifteen. He was seventeen then, and far too old for such a child. But the summer she was sixteen, she was looking not so much like a child anymore. And by her seventeenth summer she was so beautiful that he ached every time he saw her.

Fortunately or unfortunately—he'd never been able to decide which—Darcy had wanted him, too. They'd spent the entire summer watching each other sideways during the day when other people were around, and drawing together like magnets in the dark shadows of night. Sharing their inner selves, their dreams, planning a life together...and ultimately, making slow, sweet, incredible love. Until they'd gotten caught, that is.

Then she left and never came back. He never forgot her, never stopped comparing other women to her. For a long time he'd kept to himself, avoiding all romantic entanglements. But the glow of that summer romance had worn off eventually, and when he'd met a town girl named Maura Kinney, who was available and willing, he hadn't bothered to resist.

When Maura had told him she was pregnant, he'd done the right thing and married her. Why not? Maybe he *was* still thinking of Darcy, but Darcy had married some high rider in the East and was, presumably, going to live happily ever after with him.

He took a deep breath and then let it out, trying to relax his tense shoulders and neck. He still remembered the long months of wishing Darcy would come back, but not daring to ask Ken about her. He should have asked anyway, he realized now. But the boy he'd been was so cowed by the powerful R. Kenneth Beckett that he hadn't dared let anyone know the depth of his feelings for the great man's granddaughter. Hell, he'd been lucky to be able to hold on to his job. In those days, it wasn't so easy to find good work that paid a fair wage; he couldn't risk it.

Instead, he'd hidden his feelings. After all, he was young and he knew it. He thought surely his crush on Darcy would fade. It did, to an extent, when he wrote to her and didn't get an answer. He even wrote a second time, just in case the first letter had been lost. Then a third time. Then he gave up. And he'd gone to so much trouble to get the address from Kenneth's book without the old man knowing it, too.

Joe sighed, remembering. Eventually he'd started a life with another woman and his unborn child. He'd never truly been in love with Maura, but she'd been his friend. When she'd died after a short illness a couple of years ago, it had been a blow. Together they'd worked to build a life. When she died he'd had to start all over again.

He fastened his eyes on the route ahead. The old Watson place, a broken ruin of a house, was up there on the right. Almost home. The T.L. Ranch. He did this drive every day, but today, with the lawyer's meeting pending, it felt completely different—different because when he arrived at the ranch he'd get out of the car and be face to face again with Darcy Beckett.

He'd been waiting for this day for a long time. Rosanna Kinney, his late wife's sister, had been hounding him for the past eight months to get on out to her Oklahoma ranch and take over as foreman.

He would have refused flat out except that Rosanna had paid a large balance of Maura's hospital bills, and now Joe felt indebted to her. If Maura had told him about the loan before it was too late—heck, if she'd told him about the *necessity* of getting the loan—he would have done something else, anything else, to get the money.

But Maura hadn't told him, and so he didn't find out until after the funeral.

Rosanna proposed that he pay back the twenty-thousand dollars in sweat equity. Besides, she pointed out, Ricky and Joe needed a *home,* not just a place to live and work. Joe said he'd come after his ailing employer no longer needed him. Well, Kenneth Beckett no longer needed Joe or anyone else.

Now Joe had a five-year plan to work off his debt to his sister-in-law and save enough to start his own ranch in Wyoming. He'd already picked the spot. It was great land and underdeveloped. It would come cheap. With what he had saved now, and what he'd accumulate in the next five years in Oklahoma, he would be set.

He'd even been feeling optimistic about it lately. It figured that Darcy would show up now, just to throw him off.

But it was temporary. He was leaving for Oklahoma; it was part of The Plan. Until recently that plan had been unappealing to him, but now it was starting to seem like a really good idea. After today's meeting, Joe would have no more excuses for remaining in Holt.

He glanced back at Darcy. Suddenly it seemed that the sooner he got out, the better it would be for him. Falling for Darcy Beckett again was one mistake this foolish cowboy couldn't afford to make again.

Chapter Two

Darcy rounded a corner, still following the pickup and thinking about the old days. She could see Joe in her mind's eye, a little younger, a little thinner and a bit more baby-faced...but as devastatingly handsome as he was today. She never dreamed he'd still be working at the ranch. For years she'd felt guilty about the fact that he'd probably been fired; now it turned out that he never had been.

But her grandfather had been so angry! Once he'd learned of their secret trysts, he'd sent Darcy straight home, even though it was only the beginning of August. She'd assumed Joe had been sent on his way, too, especially when her letters had gone unanswered.

Now that she thought about it, though, it figured that he hadn't been. R. Kenneth Beckett's world was a man's world. Always had been. She could see it now: Joe had been given a warning and a wink.

She turned into the driveway, and the ranch spread out before her. Her heart soared. Acres and acres of sharply angled hills, dotted with horses of all sizes and colors, cradled the beloved house in a valley.

It didn't look much like a ranch, apart from the horses on the hill. It never had. The ranch had been built by a Swiss settler centuries before, and to Darcy the old European styling had always seemed like the setting for a fairy tale.

The house was large, with pointed gables and shady eaves. Thick vines climbed the wall and snaked across the front, netting the building's facade like a spider web. The windows were beveled lead glass with diagonals of iron bar slashing it into diamonds. The window sills, however, were scaly with peeling paint. Closer inspection revealed two of the windows on the far corner of the house were broken, and Darcy could clearly see boards behind several others.

When had that happened? Grandfather had always taken great pride in his home. There had never been a chip of paint missing, much less scales of it peeling off.

Darcy swallowed a lump in her throat. If she'd known he was ill, if she'd known that the house had practically fallen to ruin, would she have tried one more time? Yes, a melancholy voice inside her said, of course I would have. Another question followed quickly: Would *he* have responded with more warmth if he'd known their time for reconciliation was drawing to a close?

Apparently not. After all, he *had* known he was ill, and yet he had neither contacted her nor had anyone else do so.

Bullheaded to the bitter end.

She tightened her hands on the steering wheel. It was more comfortable to be angry with him than to miss him. There was no point in mulling over the past.

Darcy parked the car next to the pickup truck and got out warily, watching Joe Tyler from the corner of her eye.

Joe raised his eyebrow. "You ready?" He gestured toward the house.

Darcy straightened and kept walking. "Yes, I am."

"You don't look ready. You look like you've been crying. Are you okay?"

"Yes, of course I'm okay." She sniffed and hated herself for the giveaway. "It's just hay fever. I always have hay fever when I come here." She walked quickly toward the front door.

He followed.

Darcy hesitated at the door. She had always just walked right in, but that had been a very long time ago. She wasn't at all sure whom she'd find in the house now or what they would expect of her.

She pushed the doorbell and waited, trying to ignore the fact that Joe Tyler was standing close behind her. Right— as if anyone could ignore such a presence. For one thing, he smelled fantastic. She could detect a hint of sweet laundry detergent or fabric softener mingling with the crisp masculine scent of aftershave. It was a combination that tempted her to lean back into him, as if collapsing into a freshly made bed.

Heat pulsated from him right through the gauzy batiste of her pantsuit. His proximity felt uncomfortably...what was the word? *Intimate* flew to mind. The heat that passed from him to her felt intimate.

This foolish line of thinking was getting her nowhere. A long time ago she and Joe had shared a predictable teenage curiosity about each other. Nothing more, she insisted silently. It was a lifetime ago, and Darcy had been married and divorced since then, had gone from carefree wealth to economic struggle. Now she knew that following the lead of sexual chemistry could only result in disaster.

There was no way she was going to make *that* mistake again.

"Why don't you just go on in?" Joe reached past her toward the door. His arm brushed against her shoulder and left a burning spot on her skin.

"It's not my home." Although it was the closest thing she'd ever had.

"At the moment, it's no one's home, and I don't want to stand here all day while you ring the bell." He stepped around her and pushed the door open. "The Coxes are too deaf to hear it these days anyway."

"The Coxes?" She remembered Anthea, the kind woman who worked as the housekeeper, and her husband, Hank, who was the family driver. "Are they still here?"

"For the time being." He hesitated, then added gently, "It'll be a short reunion. They're getting ready to leave for Florida."

"When?"

"I'm not sure. This week sometime."

It was Darcy's second encounter today with the living past, and the second time she felt her fond memories meant more than the truth did. "Is anyone else still here? Anyone I might know?"

Joe was quick to shake his head. "There's no one here at all beyond some hired day help. The guys you knew are all long gone. The last of them was Skip Morton and he left—" he paused to think "—well, it must be nearly a year now."

"Oh, no." Darcy was filled with apprehension. She was walking into a situation that was even more unfamiliar than she'd anticipated.

"Things really changed over the past few years, Darce, and not for the best."

"Oh." Darcy didn't know what else to say. She'd had such happy times here as a child. When she went in this door, what changed vision of the past would confront her? She hesitated, almost afraid to disturb her memories.

"Let's go." Joe guided her through the front door into the wooden entryway. "Like I said, it's a little different since you were here last. Toward the end, your grandfather was too ill to do much with the place and too poor to hire someone else to do it for him."

"But you said he had hired help."

Joe shook his head. "Just a few men. All together we have our hands full just dealing with the livestock."

A door at the end of the hall creaked open before Darcy could reply.

"Joe? Is that you?" An elderly man bustled down the hall toward them. "How are you, son? Didn't recognize you from back there without my glasses on. How's Ricky?"

Darcy felt Joe glance at her quickly. Who was Ricky? she wondered. Another ranch hand? Was someone else requested at the reading of Grandfather's will?

"Just getting over a cold, but he's all right," Joe said. He took off his hat and tossed it onto the foyer table. His hair was dark and gleaming. "How are you and the missus?"

"Fine, fine." Hank turned his gaze to Darcy. "My stars, this isn't Little Darcy, is it?"

"Not so little anymore." She smiled, but tears burned behind her eyes. Hank had aged thirty years in the last ten, but he was still wonderfully familiar. He made the place feel like home in a way that no one else could. "I'm awfully glad to see you, Hank.'' Impulsively she went to him and gave the frail body a hug. Hank returned the hug with the warm kindness she remembered.

"Wait 'til Anthea sees you.'' He hesitated and appeared to think that over before saying, "She'll be so sorry it's just to say good-bye.''

"I can't wait to see her,'' Darcy said, trepidation weakening her words.

"You waited ten years,'' Joe said quietly.

Darcy bristled.

"Come right this way,'' Hank Cox said, walking through a heavy oak doorway to the left.

Neither Darcy nor Joe moved. They stood facing each other like boxers in opposite corners of the ring.

"What did you mean, 'you waited ten years'?'' she demanded.

"Just that your grandfather could have used your help over the past few years, and if you weren't so bull-headed—''

"*Me* bullheaded? What about *him?*''

"Both of you. Not that it's any of my business,'' he added as an afterthought.

"It certainly isn't.'' She was sorely tempted to spit the truth right into Joe Tyler's condescending face, but it was none of his business. Let him think the worst of her—what did she care?

He stood for a moment with his eyes fixed on her, and his enviably sculpted mouth quirked into the half smile she'd noticed earlier. "Sweetheart, you're *way* too uptight.''

"Don't call me 'sweetheart.'''

"See?''

She felt her face flush. "You have no right to speak to me that way."

"You didn't used to feel that way."

Exactly three hard, solid heartbeats passed before she managed to say, "I don't know what you're talking about." His casual approach to what had meant so much to her was humiliating.

He stopped and turned back to her. Suddenly his hair looked darker—if that was possible—and his eyes looked like blue stormclouds. And his mouth—that sensually curved mouth; it was really starting to get on Darcy's nerves—was quirked, openly mocking. "You didn't *used* to mind one bit when I called you my sweetheart. Or have you forgotten?"

"There's nothing to forget," she answered, refusing to be bowled over by him. She raised her chin.

He gave a quick jerk of his head and sucked air in through his teeth. "Are you challenging me, Darcy?"

"To do what?" Darcy asked, deliberately misunderstanding.

He didn't miss a beat. "To make a more lasting impression on your memory."

Part of her wanted to slap that complacent smirk right off his face, but at the moment she felt too weak and tingly to move. Once she had enjoyed this sensation. Now she hated it.

"If you're ready…" Hank Cox returned to the doorway with a puzzled frown and swept a hand toward the other room. Darcy had almost forgotten he was waiting. She strode into the library and sat down in an embroidered antique chair.

The room was actually in pretty good shape, except for

some chips in the built-in bookshelves and a few pieces of old furniture that had seen better days.

A little gray-haired woman who would have been perfectly cast as Mrs. Claus approached with teapot in hand but not a shred of recognition in her eye. "I'm Anthea Cox, and I'm delighted to meet you."

"It's me, Anthea. Darcy." She stared hard into the woman's eyes, willing her to remember. "Darcy Beckett."

"Oh, my." Anthea put a hand to her chest. "Little Darcy—is it really you?"

Darcy felt tears prick her eyes. "Yes. It's been a long time."

"It certainly has," the woman answered, her voice wavering with emotion. "Far too long." She walked over and reached her hand out to touch Darcy's cheek. "How lovely you've turned out to be. I always knew you would."

"Th-thanks," Darcy said awkwardly, giving Anthea a quick embrace. She was keenly aware of Joe, standing nearby, listening.

"How about a nice cup of tea?" Anthea asked. "I remember how you like it, with lots of sugar and cream."

Her sugar and cream days had been over for a long time, but Darcy saw it was important to Anthea and said, "How kind. I'd love some." Seeing that Anthea's hands shook with age, Darcy reached out to help, but the older woman didn't notice.

"Nothing quite like a nice cuppa to cure what ails you," Anthea murmured. She'd always said that, but Darcy didn't believe it anymore.

Darcy watched the thin trickle of tea dance in and around the cup as Anthea poured unsteadily.

"Dear, did you see that Joe is here, too?" Hank Cox asked from across the room.

Anthea Cox looked up. The teapot shifted position but continued to pour, now onto the table, as she said, "Well, Joseph, how nice—"

"Excuse me, Anthea," Darcy said, reaching for the teapot. The older woman apparently didn't hear her, because just as Darcy was about to grasp the teapot Anthea shifted both her gaze and the teapot back to Darcy.

"Mr. Beckett would have been so pleased that you've come back at last," she said faintly to Darcy, who was frantically setting empty tea cups under the trickling stream.

Joe walked over and took the pot from Anthea Cox, saying, "I was just telling Darcy myself what a shame it was that she waited so long to come back."

Darcy looked daggers at him. She wanted to tell him that the responsibility for her absence was not hers alone, but she knew it would sound petty. If he remembered that she'd given him her virginity, it certainly didn't seem to mean much to him now. "Well, our past doesn't mean that much to me, either," she contended, looking down at her shoes. She didn't realize she'd spoken the words aloud until she looked up.

Three surprised gazes landed on her like bugs.

"What do you mean, dear?" Anthea asked.

A long moment of silence followed.

"I mean," Darcy stammered, "I mean that the past is the past, and there's no point in regretting it now." She leveled her gaze on Joe. "No matter how much I might want to."

"Quite so," Anthea agreed. "Quite so."

There was a strained silence, but before the awkwardness became torturous a man walked into the room wearing a fine gray pinstripe suit and carrying a thin leather briefcase. "I'm sorry I'm late." He gave a cursory nod to everyone in the room, then settled his gaze on Darcy and Joe. "I'm Edward Connor, Mr. Beckett's attorney. You must be Ms. Beckett and Mr. Tyler."

They both nodded.

"Good. Then we'll sort out the future of the True Love Ranch."

"The *True Love* Ranch?" Darcy repeated incredulously. "What's that?"

"*This* is that," Joe answered. "Didn't you know?"

"The T.L. Ranch...you're saying that stands for *True Love?*"

Joe looked at her strangely. "Yeah. You must have known that."

She shook her head, trying to make sense of the sentimental name her grandfather had given to his home. "I can't believe it."

From the top shelf Joe took the baseball that had been signed to her grandfather by Babe Ruth and tossed it in the air. "It's absolutely true." He caught the ball.

"Does anyone know where the name came from?"

"Well, yeah. He named it in honor of his wife," Joe said simply.

"What?"

"Your grandfather. He named it in honor of your grandmother."

"You must be mistaken."

Joe shook his head and tossed the ball again. "Nope. He told me so himself. Why the shock? Can't you believe the old guy loved his wife?"

"Frankly, no."

"Come on, Darce," Joe said, using the old nickname he'd given her.

"I never thought he loved anyone."

Joe's look hardened. "He loved you, and you know it."

She gave a wry laugh, ignoring the increasingly impatient lawyer and the increasingly confused Coxes. "That's why he refused to speak to me when I married a man he didn't approve of."

"He was right, wasn't he?"

"That's not the point."

"No," Joe agreed, apparently no more concerned about the others in the room than Darcy was. "It's not. He was worried about you. I think it was the only way he could think of to make you reconsider your decision."

"At some point he must have realized it wasn't working."

Joe shrugged. "You Becketts are so inflexible sometimes. He probably didn't know how to approach you anymore than you knew how to approach him."

Just then the lawyer cleared his throat. "Excuse me, I just have some papers here for your signatures, and then I think we'll be ready to go," he said.

"Not that all of that is any of my business," Joe went on to Darcy, "but—"

Darcy's reply was pointed. "No, it *isn't* any of your business."

The lawyer went to a broad rolltop desk that Darcy remembered from childhood. It was an impressive piece of artistry, walnut stained to a deep amber sheen. Inside, she knew, it had all sorts of secret drawers and shelves. As a child she had loved playing with it.

No one spoke as the lawyer unsnapped the fasteners on his briefcase and pulled out a pile of papers.

"Mr. Tyler, Ms. Beckett, Mr. Beckett left the sum of $20,000 to Mr. and Mrs. Cox for their years of faithful duty. That is the whole of Mr. Beckett's liquid assets. What remains, however, is this property, consisting of the house and everything in it, and one thousand acres of surrounding property.''

Darcy slipped a peek at Joe. What was *he* really doing here? Was there a token bequest of some favorite paperweight or money clip or something? How close had he and her grandfather become before the older man had died?

That question was quickly replaced by another, more fearful one: What had *she* been asked here for?

Grandfather couldn't have left anything to her. Some cruel part of her mind told her that maybe he'd left her some final token of disapproval, but that wouldn't have been like him. He'd been a hardheaded man, sure of what was right and what was wrong to his way of thinking, but she couldn't believe he'd ever deliberately set out to hurt her. He certainly wouldn't do that now, as his final act.

Darcy found herself kneading her hands in her lap. She wished the lawyer would just get on with it.

''Now for the rest of the estate,'' Edward Connor continued, as if in answer to her thoughts. He looked from Darcy to Joe, and back again. ''Mr. Beckett left the property to the two of you—Mr. Tyler, Ms. Beckett—to be shared equally.''

Darcy gasped.

Joe dropped the baseball.

''What do you mean 'shared equally'?'' Darcy asked.

The attorney gazed at her impassively. ''As of this moment, you each have an equal share in True Love Ranch.''

Chapter Three

"Wait a minute," Darcy interrupted. "The ranch is going to the two of us? Joe and me? That has to be a mistake."

"It doesn't sound right to me, either," Joe said, exchanging a quick glance with Darcy. "This is Mr. Beckett's granddaughter. I was just a friend. An employee, in fact. Are you sure you've read that correctly?"

The lawyer looked at them both through hooded eyes. "I don't make mistakes."

Darcy privately thought the mistake might be that a share in the ranch had been left to her at all.

The lawyer continued as though he hadn't just dropped a bombshell. "The property has been left to both of you, with some conditions attached."

"Conditions?" Darcy echoed.

He gave a curt nod. "Now, these papers are duplicates for each of you to sign. They say only that you agree to sharing the ranch fifty-fifty—"

"What if we don't?" Darcy asked.

Silence expanded and filled the room.

Darcy tried to ignore Joe's burning gaze on her. "I'm just wondering. I mean, this is absurd. What—how—when did my grandfather draw up this will?"

The lawyer looked at his papers and read the date.

"The day after I got married," Darcy said, more to herself than to anyone else in the room. "I don't understand. Why did he do this?"

"Ms. Beckett, I have no explanations for why your grandfather bequeathed his estate as he did. I can only tell you that this is what he intended, and that you have no legal grounds for objection. I might just add that this is an extremely valuable property, and owning half of it is considerably better than owning none at all."

"I realize that, of course," Darcy said hurriedly. "I'm not complaining—"

The lawyer tapped his pen on the desk. "I'd like to continue now, so you two can sign the papers and take ownership—"

"Did he say *anything* that might explain this decision?" Darcy asked.

"He did not. May I continue?"

She nodded weakly. Once upon a time, this would have been a dream come true. She and Joe had talked about having a place just like this for themselves someday. They'd talked of getting married, she remembered bitterly. Of having a home, children, a life together.

It had taken Darcy a very long time to get over that dream. How ironic that part of it should be coming true now.

"If you could both just sign here," the lawyer said,

laying two sheets of paper on the desk and holding out pens for Darcy and Joe.

Darcy suddenly realized that Joe hadn't moved since hearing the news.

"What's the matter, Joe?" she asked wryly. "This can't be such a surprise to you. After all, you've been here, with him, for quite some time now."

He shook his head. "Darcy, this is as much of a shock to me as it is to you. I have other plans. I was getting ready to leave Colorado."

"Meaning you don't *want* half this place?"

"Meaning I'm not at all sure how this fits in." He looked into her eyes, searchingly. "I suppose you'll be contesting the will?"

"Why?"

He shrugged. "To change the terms?"

"You mean to cut you out." When he didn't answer, she went on. "Honestly, Joe, I'm grateful that my grandfather left me anything. If he wanted you to have half of this place, or the proceeds from half, who am I to say that's wrong? My personal feelings about you are irrelevant."

He eyed her silently for a few moments, then seemed lost in his thoughts again.

"We do need to get those signatures," the lawyer prompted them impatiently.

As she took a pen, Darcy was very aware of Joe's lean physique beside her, but she didn't risk a glance at him.

"We'd like to read this over before signing," Joe said.

Following his lead, Darcy read the document then lifted her gaze to Joe's.

"I don't have a problem signing it," Joe said.

"Me, neither."

They signed.

As Edward Connor was about to hand over the keys, Hank Cox cleared his throat and said quietly, "Did you have them sign the *other* part?"

"Ah, yes," the lawyer said. "The addendum. I was about to get to that." He reached into another pocket of his case and took out two single sheets.

"What's this?" Joe asked, taking one.

"These are the conditions I referred to earlier."

Joe looked the document over. Then, with a dramatic frown, he asked, "Is this necessary?"

"What?" Darcy reached for the paper with a sinking heart. "Is what necessary?"

The lawyer's grave nod reminded Darcy of the nod Wilton Hammersmith had given her four years ago after telling Darcy her husband had gone to South America with the remainder of her trust fund.

"Those are the terms Mr. Beckett laid out," Edward Connor stated.

"What terms?" Darcy asked, frantically scanning the paper, then looking at the attorney. "What is this?"

Edward Connor took a breath and gave just the smallest shrug before saying, "This is a simple addendum stating that you will both live on the property, and agree not to sell any part of the stated property—either to each other or to another party—for a period of two months from this date."

"I can't stay for two months!" Darcy and Joe said simultaneously, then glanced at each other.

"Where are you going?" Joe asked, looking surprised.

"I'm going to California. There's a job waiting for me there."

He raised his eyebrows. "So you weren't planning on staying here at all?"

She tried to give a laugh, but it came out as a quick rush of air. "Absolutely not."

"That's typical, always hopping from place to place."

"I have no intention of 'hopping from place to place' anymore. I'm settling down in California, and with any luck at all I'll never leave again." She frowned. "Anyway, you've been here for ten years, why can't *you* stay?"

"I've got to get to Oklahoma. I've also got a job waiting."

Darcy turned to the lawyer. "Neither one of us can stay."

He lifted his shoulders slightly. "I'm afraid those are the terms."

"When was that addendum drawn up?" Darcy asked.

The lawyer looked at the paper and slid his glasses down his nose to read it. "September the nineteenth," he answered.

"Hmm."

"That date significant to you?" Joe asked.

Her stomach knotted. September the nineteenth was her birthday. Did Joe remember that? Did he remember how they'd planned to marry on that day ten years ago? Was he testing her, to gauge her reaction?

She doubted it. He probably didn't remember things nearly as keenly as she did. If he had any idea of the pain those memories could still inflict...well, obviously he didn't have any idea. He didn't care the way she did. Obviously he never had. So the irony of the date would undoubtedly be lost on him.

She met his eyes evenly. "It was the day after my divorce became final," she said dully.

"Hmm," murmured Joe.

"First the True Love and now this...this *forcing* you

and me to be together after everything that happened.'' Darcy took a slow breath, considering. ''I'm starting to wonder if my grandfather had a well-hidden romantic side, or if he was just a controlling old curmudgeon.''

''Is it impossible to imagine he might have had other reasons?'' Joe asked. ''Like maybe he cared about us both and couldn't decide what else to do?''

She leveled her gaze on Joe again. ''It's no secret that my family isn't exactly what you'd call close.''

He nodded. ''I always thought that was a shame.''

''It suits us,'' she answered. ''We don't like to be encumbered with familial responsibilities.''

He nodded again but said nothing. Darcy thought she saw pity in his eyes. He knew too much about her, even that her mother had run off with a polo player when Darcy was ten, and that they'd never heard from her again, except for the odd impersonal Christmas card. Darcy had told that story to Joe ages ago in a moment of weakness, but she could see he was thinking about it now and, worse, feeling sorry for her.

Oh, who was she kidding? Darcy was the one feeling sorry. Sorry that the man who had meant so much to her as a child was dead, and that there was no way she could pull back the years that had been wasted. She'd tried to contact him, certainly, but maybe she could have tried harder. Maybe she should have tried longer. Maybe, maybe, maybe....

''Are you in agreement with the terms?'' the lawyer asked sharply. ''I do have another appointment to make.''

Joe looked at Darcy and cocked his head. ''Do you think you can put your job off for a couple of months?'' He paused. ''I think I can.''

She sighed. "I can too." She looked at the lawyer. "I guess we'll give it a try."

With a nod, the lawyer made some scribbles on the papers in front of him.

"It's going to be worth it," Joe said.

Worth it or not, I'm not ready to give it up, Darcy thought. But she didn't voice it. Instead she said, "I want to take a look around."

She glanced at her watch so that Joe wouldn't see the tears in her eyes. "Excuse me."

She had barely reached the hall when she felt Joe's hand on her arm. "Darcy, what's the matter?"

She took a quick swipe at her eyes with the back of her hand. "Nothing. I'm just tired."

He cocked his head. "Really."

"I'm fine." She gave a quick sniff. "I told you, I have allergies."

"I think you're upset that Ken left part of this place to me."

"That's not true! I'm not—"

"Come on, who wouldn't be?"

The melancholy left her and she was once again riled at Joe. "You always think you can read my mind."

"I usually can."

"It's been years since you've even had the chance to guess. How could you possibly know what I'm thinking?"

He remained irritatingly calm. "Because what you're thinking is usually written all over you face, for anyone with eyes to see."

"Then maybe it's time you think about getting some glasses, because you're wrong."

"I am?"

"Completely. You really want to know what I think?"

"Yeah."

"I think there's no way this could work. I don't see how we can live here together. Maybe we should consult another lawyer, maybe find out if there's some loophole that would enable one of us to live somewhere else." She looked at him and added quickly, "Oh, don't worry, I'm not trying to get your half for myself. It's right that Grandfather should have left you something. I just wish he'd done it a little less awkwardly."

Joe gave a nod but said nothing.

"Anyway, if I get another lawyer—"

Joe stopped her. "If you get another lawyer involved, that's going to cost money and time that I don't think either one of us can spare."

"But, Joe—" she shook her head "—we can't seriously entertain the idea of living here together."

"We have to." His voice softened fractionally, but she heard the anxiety in it. "This is an amazing opportunity, at least for me."

"I need it, too," Darcy said softly.

He hesitated for a moment. "I don't know about you, but I don't have time to monkey with long-shot loopholes. Two months isn't *that* long."

"I don't know…"

He eyed her with suspicion. "What are you so worried about? You think your virtue is at risk with me?"

But she wondered if she could resist him, if it ever came to that. At close quarters, he still turned her insides to melted butter. And living together on the ranch, they'd be in close quarters much of the time. "I'm not worried about anything. I just don't think we're ideally suited as roommates—"

"Listen." This time his voice had a definite edge to it.

"You're going to have to get used to this—and fast. So here's what I propose. We stay on for the two months and fix the place up as inexpensively as possible—that's going to mean getting a little dirt under those manicured fingernails of yours—then we sell it at the end of the term. We'll split the profit fifty-fifty, less expenses. Do you agree?"

"I— I—"

"You're not very good with commitment, are you?"

"I do." Her head was swimming. She stood and walked a small circle in front of her chair. "I mean, I *am*. I mean, I do agree to the deal, and I am good with commitment. Not that it's any of your business."

"It is now," he said easily. "We'll have to draw up a contract, of course."

"A *contract*?"

"You'd prefer a handshake, I suppose."

"You'd prefer blood, I suppose."

"Let's stick with a contract."

"And what, exactly, will it say?"

"It will say that we will both stay on for two months to meet the terms of your grandfather's addendum, so that *you* don't leave and mess everything up for me. Then, at the end of the term, we sell the ranch and go our separate ways. For good."

It took a moment for the answer to make it to her lips. "Fine."

He extended his hand. "Then we're agreed?"

She hesitated for a moment, then took his hand. "Agreed." She felt as if an electric current were traveling from his flesh to hers, and wondered if he felt it, too.

He seemed to hold her hand an extra moment before letting go. "Good."

Darcy took a long breath, hoping he wouldn't see how his touch had affected her. "I'm going out now."

He held her gaze. "I'll go back in and have Connor draw up a contract for the two of us. Okay?" He turned and walked back to the library.

"Don't go too far," he said, glancing over his shoulder. "I'll need you to sign before you change your mind."

As soon as the crisp November air hit her skin, Darcy felt better. She breathed deeply, inhaling the wintery scent of burning wood and cold air. The sky had turned steel gray overhead, threatening rain, but she didn't care. She took long aimless strides, willing her heartbeat to return to normal.

I'll need you to sign before you change your mind, Joe had said. As if she had the luxury of that kind of choice.

It had been a long road back to the T.L. Ranch, she thought as she found herself in front of the horse paddock. A dark chestnut horse munching on hay across the paddock lifted its head briefly, then resumed eating.

Darcy clamped her hands on the cold wooden fence, noting that it was in desperate need of a coat of paint. She ran her fingertips across the wood and wondered if she was the last person to have painted it. It would have been eleven or twelve years ago now, but from the looks of the fence, that was possible.

She sighed and leaned against the fence. It seemed she was the only one in her family who ever lamented the estrangement among them. She thought about calling her mother now but nixed the idea quickly. They hadn't spoken in six years. Perhaps the worst part of it was that they hadn't even had a falling out. It was just distance, emotional and geographical, that kept them apart.

Fifteen years had gone by since her father's death. She'd lost touch with her various stepfathers along the way as well. Somehow, while her grandfather had been alive, she'd always felt as if maybe there was a connection out there, as if maybe they would make up someday and be close the way they used to be. Now that was impossible. Now there was no one to connect with.

She was alone.

Except for Tyler. She tried to dismiss his image, but couldn't. He'd meant so much to her once. She had thought she'd gotten over him. She had thought her anger had obliterated any remaining affection, but seeing him face to face, his bone-melting good looks cast their spell over her again. There was also a strangely comforting familiarity about him, despite all the years they'd been apart. He was…*home* somehow, at least as close to home as she had ever known, and she wanted to run to him as much as she wanted to run away from him.

A rumbling engine fifty yards away caught her attention, and she turned. A school bus lumbered to a halt at the foot of the driveway. As the door opened, a small dark-haired boy, not more than five or six, stepped off the bus. His bright red coat was unzipped and gaping open. In one hand he clutched a lunch box and in the other what looked like a handful of papers.

Darcy pushed off the fence and walked toward the bus, grateful for something to get her mind off Joe. But a school bus? There had to be a mistake. The child didn't belong here, and there wasn't another house for at least a mile. Joe might know who the child was. But there was no time to find Joe.

The bus door started to close, and Darcy ran toward it. "Wait!" she cried.

The door banged shut.

The boy looked at her, then behind him at the bus that had already begun to rumble down the street.

"Don't worry," Darcy panted when she got to the boy. "We'll get you home." She swallowed and tried to catch her breath. "What's your name?"

"Rick," the boy said importantly. He held up a piece of newsprint blotched with watercolor paint. In the bottom right corner an adult had written "Ricky."

"Okay, Rick. What's your last name?"

He thrust the painting toward her. "I did this myself. Nobody helped me."

Darcy remembered her own early artistic attempts, and her parents' painful lack of interest. "Let me see. I like your picture, Rick. What's your last name, honey?"

"You want it? Here." He pressed the paper into her hand.

It wasn't quite dry, she noticed. "Thank you, Rick." She reached for his hand. "Why don't you come in the house with me, and we'll use the telephone to call your parents, okay?"

"I'm not allowed in the big house without my daddy. I'm six years old. I can't go anywhere by myself until I'm eighteen. My daddy said so."

Darcy laughed in spite of herself. "Okay, well, your daddy isn't here so I'm sure it'll be okay for you to go with another grown-up who is going to help you get home."

He looked dubious. "Daddy said I shouldn't go anywhere with strangers."

She sighed. "And Daddy is absolutely right. But your bus driver left you at the wrong place and I'm going to help you get home. I'm sure your mother would want me to do that.''

"I don't have a mother," the boy said matter-of-factly. "My mom's dead. I don't remember her."

"Oh. I'm sorry." Darcy's chest tightened. She looked at the boy walking along beside her, his long eyelashes sweeping down toward pale, freckled cheeks. For a wild instant she wished she were this appealing child's mother. "Okay, then, what's your daddy's name?"

"It's Joseph."

"Joseph," she repeated. Her heart nearly stopped. No way. It was impossible.

The child beamed up at her. "That's Jesus' father's name. Joseph. We're doing a play about Jesus at my school."

Had the child confused his own father with the father in the play? "I see. But what's *your* father's name?"

"I told you. Joseph." Then, looking at the barn, he suddenly cried, "There's Chocolate Chip!"

She followed the line of his gaze but saw nothing unusual.

"Where?"

"There." He pointed a chubby finger at the horse eating hay in the paddock. It occurred to her that there should be a glove or a mitten on that hand. "That's Chocolate Chip right there. The horsey."

"Is that right? How do you know that?"

"My dad trained him." He puffed his chest up with six-year-old pride. "He let me name him, though."

Once again, Darcy felt a strange tingling in her chest. "Your daddy trained him?"

"Yup. Where *is* Daddy? He's s'posed to meet me at the bus. Did he tell you to meet me instead?"

"No," she said cautiously. "Rick, who is your daddy?"

"Why don't you ask him yourself?" a deep voice asked behind her.

She wheeled around and found herself face to face with Joe.

Chapter Four

"**D**addy!" the boy shrieked, and jumped into Joe's arms.

Darcy's mouth dropped open. "You're…" She pointed to Rick. "He's your…your *son?*"

Joe laughed. "Yes. Ricky, this is Darcy Beckett. Darcy, Richard Michael Tyler."

"How do you do?" the boy said formally, with a quick glance at his father.

"Your hand," Joe whispered with a smile.

"Oh." Ricky thrust his hand out. "How do you do?"

Darcy took his hand in hers, feeling as if she were in a dream. "How do you do?" she replied with as much sobriety as she could muster. "You're very polite."

"I have to be," the boy grumbled. "Who is she?" he asked Joe in a stage whisper.

"Darcy is Mr. Beckett's granddaughter. She'll be staying here with us for awhile."

"Goodie! I like her."

Joe put the boy down and gave him a light pat on the behind. "You run on into the house now and wash up. Then you can have a piece of cheese from the fridge, okay?"

"'Kay." The boy ran off without a backward glance.

"I had no idea," Darcy said. As she watched Joe smile his pirate smile, she found it impossible to imagine this gorgeous, rakish former hell-raiser as a father. "I don't know what to say."

"Should I take this to mean you don't see me as the ideal dad?" he asked, humor warming his voice.

"Frankly, I'm just stunned. It hadn't occurred to me—"

"I understand."

"It's almost impossible to think of you—"

"Darcy!"

She met his gaze, flustered. "Yes?"

"It's okay. I have a son. Get over it now." He held her gaze a moment longer, then added, "I lost my wife a few years back."

"Ricky mentioned that. I'm sorry. I—" She shrugged helplessly. This image of Joe as a father didn't fit in at all with her already conflicting feelings for him. "Look, I didn't mean to insult you."

"It's okay. Really." He hooked his thumbs in his belt loops. "There's no reason you should have known, being out of touch like you were."

"It must be hard."

"It's been a long time," he said, with no visible emotion. "I'm used to it now. I think Ricky could use a mother sometimes, but he doesn't remember her well enough to feel bad about it. I think that's for the best."

Darcy nodded mutely.

"I mean it," he said, with a smile that crinkled at the

corners of his eyes. "You don't have to look so stricken. We're okay."

She tried to smile. "Do you have any more? Kids, I mean."

"Nope. You've met everyone now."

"He's adorable."

Joe gave a quick, proud smile. "He's a good kid."

An awkward silence stretched between them.

"I'd better go in," Darcy said at last. She wanted to reach out to him, to say something comforting about his wife's death, his years as a single father—which must have been tough for him in the beginning at least—but nothing came to mind. "I've got to get to know my surroundings again."

"We'll be in the guest house if you need anything."

"The guest house?"

"By the barns."

For a split second she was relieved. They wouldn't have to share living quarters. Then she remembered the impersonal barracks where all the ranch hands had lived together. "That's no place for a child," she admonished.

"It is now," he assured her.

"That barracks? With all those other men?"

"Those guys are long gone, remember? The help we have now come in during the day and leave at night. It's just Ricky and me there now."

"I still can't see that as a good place for a child," Darcy insisted. She wasn't at all sure Joe and her grandfather would have a clue as to what was appropriate surroundings for a child.

Not that she did. She had even less experience with children than either one of them.

"Don't worry about it. You've been gone a long time. Things have changed."

She nodded.

"See you later then, eh, partner?" He held out his hand.

Two hours ago she'd been very apprehensive about this forced partnership, and now that she'd met Ricky, she felt even more confused. This was no longer just about her and Joe—there was an innocent child involved, a child who needed a home and security.

She slipped her hand into his and drew a breath at the shock of his touch. It was uncanny, the way the chemistry had remained unchanged all these years. "I hope we can make this work," she said.

"You got some reason to think it won't?"

"I've got about fifty reasons to think it won't, don't you?"

"I'm sure we can manage," Joe said, letting her hand go.

Something in his eyes made her hesitate, waiting for him to continue. When he didn't, she said, "I'm willing to give it a try if you are."

"Oh, I'm willing."

His voice was quiet, but the intent behind his words made it clear that for some reason, and no matter what those "other prospects" were that he kept alluding to, this was extremely important to him.

Darcy went in to the kitchen for a cup of coffee. She'd only been back at the ranch for a couple of hours, but she felt as if she'd been here much longer.

Anthea was in there, cleaning up in her familiar, bustling way. "Hello, Darcy. I thought you'd be out at the stables, the way you always were as a child."

"I'm not a child anymore," Darcy said, hearing a note of sadness in her own voice.

If Anthea noticed it, she was too tactful to say anything. "Your grandfather picked a good helper for you in Joe. He's always worked harder than three men."

"I think Grandfather picked Joe because he was mad at me and wanted to make sure someone else would stick around to pick on me."

Anthea laughed gently. "Now, I know for certain that's not true, and I think you know it, too. Your grandfather knew you were...fond of Joe."

Darcy eyed Anthea. How much did she know about the past?

As if reading Darcy's mind, the older woman said, "I know that boy meant a lot to you once. I saw a change in you that summer. It was as if you were becoming a woman." She stated it flatly, without the lift of a question.

She *knew,* thought Darcy.

Darcy swiped at the sudden tears in her eyes and went to the sink to fill a glass with water. "It seemed Grandfather wasn't very happy about that."

"He was sorry later. He was sorry when he saw how Joe—" She stopped abruptly.

"When Joe what?" Darcy asked, wanting to know. She turned to face Anthea. "Did Joe say something to him about me?"

"Oh, no, nothing like that." Anthea shook her head. "He had too much male pride to let anyone know how he felt, but it was obvious just the same."

Darcy didn't have a lot of faith in Anthea's speculations, but she waited for her to go on.

"I think your grandfather saw it, too." Anthea laid a hand on Darcy's shoulder. "He'd have to have been blind not to. But he didn't know how to tell you until…until now.'' She shook her head.

''*Now* it's ancient history,'' Darcy informed her. ''Joe doesn't mean anything to me anymore.''

''Is that right?''

''I barely remember him.''

''Child, I think you're fibbing to yourself. You were never the sort to have light emotions.''

Darcy swallowed hard. ''I learned.''

Anthea shook her head. ''People who feel as strongly about things as you *can't* learn not to. It's just the way you are.''

Darcy met the older woman's eyes, and tears spilled out over her cheeks. ''Isn't life a mess sometimes?'' she said, wiping the tears away.

Anthea pulled a handkerchief out of her pocket, approaching Darcy and dabbed at her eyes. ''What is it, child? What's hurting so bad now that you're finally back home?''

Darcy took the handkerchief Anthea offered her and blew her nose. ''It's nothing. It's everything.'' She sniffed and sat down at the table, head in hands. ''I feel so…strange being here. Like I want to go home, but I don't know where that is anymore. I don't think I ever knew.''

''*This* is home,'' Anthea said simply. ''This has always been your home.''

Darcy gave a derisive snort. ''This isn't home. It's a beat up old mausoleum that I'm being forced to stay in for two months when I should be going to California to *make* a home for myself.''

''You always loved it here.''

She shook her head and felt the tears sting at her eyes

again. "That was long ago. It's time for me to settle down and become a grown-up now, Anthea."

"Yes, it's time," Anthea agreed, patting Darcy's back. "It's time for you to learn that it's within your power to be home no matter where you are."

"I lost those ruby slippers a long time ago."

"Then find them," Anthea said, a slight urgency in her voice. "Don't waste your life feeling sorry for yourself. Find those ruby slippers."

"I can't—"

Anthea held up a hand. "They're here and you have to find them again, put 'em on and go dancing in them."

At the word "dancing" Darcy had a momentary vision of herself waltzing slowly around a dance floor with Joe, feeling herself at home in his strong, protective embrace. She blinked and the vision faded, like the mirage it was. Joe had already made a home with another woman, and now he was making one with his son. She didn't belong with them, Darcy reminded herself, and wondered why acknowledging such an obvious reality made her feel so terribly forlorn.

Why was it the word *home* always conjured up an image of Joe Tyler?

Chapter Five

As it was getting dark that evening, Ricky came running into the kitchen where Darcy and Anthea were having coffee.

"The fence is broken," Ricky announced breathlessly. "The horses can get out."

"Slow down, child," Anthea soothed. "What's wrong?"

A guilty expression came over his face. "I was climbing on the fence by the barn and it broke." He shoved a scraped forearm toward them as proof. "Now the horses can get out."

Darcy sprang to her feet. "Where's your dad?"

"Home."

Darcy hesitated for a moment, wondering why Ricky would have come to the big house instead of his own. Maybe it was because it was closer, she decided. Or because he was used to coming to the Coxes with his problems, just the way she used to.

Either way, she knew it couldn't be because he wanted her, although the initial idea had come to her and given her pleasure. They'd only just met.

"Show me where you mean," Darcy said, reaching for his hand. "Would you call Joe and tell him to meet us there?" she asked Anthea over her shoulder.

"I certainly will," Anthea answered, with a knowing smile.

Darcy felt she should refute the romantic notions she suspected were behind that smile, but there wasn't time.

She and Ricky rushed out to the paddock in the slanting amber sunlight. "I'm really sorry," he said. "Don't be mad at me."

"I'm not mad at you, sweetie. Don't worry about it. It could have happened to anyone." They stopped at a large gap in the fence where splintered wood lay in a pile before them. "Gosh, it's a wonder you weren't seriously hurt."

He puffed out his small chest. "I didn't even cry."

"Wow, what a big boy."

Most of the horses remained oblivious to the escape route Ricky had created. Only one of them, an old imp named Bosco, edged near. "Scat, Bosco!" Darcy waved her arms to shoo him away. "Go on now."

"You know Bosco?"

"Sure. He's been here for years."

"Me, too."

Darcy smiled. "He's been here even more years than you have." She looked toward the small house that Joe and Ricky shared, and saw Joe coming toward them carrying a toolbox.

"Here comes your dad now."

"He's been here for years, too."

She nodded. "Yes, he has."

"He says he used to want to have a ranch just like this all for himself, but now he's not so sure."

Darcy frowned. "He said that?"

Ricky nodded importantly. "But I want this ranch for *me*."

She laughed and mussed his hair. "That's exactly how I used to feel. You know, I used to come here every summer and stay for the whole time, just riding and swimming in the lake and listening to the frogs and owls singing at night."

Ricky giggled. "Frogs and owls don't sing!"

"They sure do. It may not sound like singing to us, but to them it's the most beautiful music in the world."

"I like the blues."

"Do you?" It struck her as a very strange thing for a child to like.

"Yep. Just like my dad." He paused, then asked, "What *is* the blues?"

Ah, that explained it, she thought. "It's sad music." She sighed. "I prefer the frogs."

"Kissing them?" Joe asked from behind her.

She whirled to face him, surprised. "No. Listening to them. Ricky and I were just talking about music."

"She likes to listen to frogs and owls and so do I," Ricky told him.

Joe smiled and his eyes crinkled irresistibly. "Two of a kind." He set the toolbox down and lifted a couple of boards from the fence. Examining the damage, he said, "This shouldn't be too hard to fix."

"See?" Darcy said to Ricky. "I told you it wasn't anything to worry about."

Ricky frowned and glanced at the big house. "Mr. Beckett used to get mad when things broke."

Darcy felt a pang in her chest. Obviously even Ricky, as young as he was, had witnessed her grandfather's temper. The fear she saw cross Ricky's face sent a momentary tremor of anxiety through her. She immediately recalled the last time she'd seen him.

She'd been in the kitchen with Joe. They were kissing, making grand plans for the dream of a shared future. She'd never been happier. Her life had never felt more on track. Then her grandfather had burst in, and the dream popped like a beautiful birthday balloon, leaving nothing but pitiful scraps behind.

The scene had been too ugly to dwell on. Over the years it had entered her mind a thousand times, but she always pushed it away. Kenneth shouting, her pleading, Joe trying to talk some sense into Kenneth, calm on the outside but with a barely detectable tremor in his voice. The Coxes had come running in to see what was going on, and before long it seemed as if everyone within fifty miles of the ranch was there. In fact, that probably wasn't far from accurate, since they had been holding a Fourth of July party.

The humiliation was enormous. Kenneth had gone straight to the phone and called Darcy's mother, telling her that he was sending Darcy home on the next plane. She couldn't be trusted here, he'd said. She was getting into trouble with one of the boys.

Getting into trouble. She hadn't gotten into trouble with Joe; she'd fallen in love with him. And she'd stayed that way, far longer than was healthy for her.

"He sure could yell," Ricky said, and Darcy recognized that he wasn't as afraid of her grandfather as she'd initially believed.

Unfortunately, she realized at the same moment that she

was almost as frightened of the man in memory as she had been as a teenager ten years ago.

Joe locked eyes with her. "Kenneth mellowed out a lot in the last few years." It was as though he could read her mind. The corners of his mouth hinted at a smile. "I think Ricky's thinking of a time when the old guy spilled hot coffee on himself."

"He yelled *so loud*," Ricky said, full of animation. "He *threw* the cup across the room and it broke all over the place and then he said a really bad word."

She could well imagine. Kenneth had a veritable dictionary in his head of really bad words for when he was angry. "Did it scare you?" she asked sympathetically.

"Nah. It was funny." He chuckled, proving it.

Darcy looked to Joe and he shrugged. "Scared *me*," he said, with that devastating smile.

Suddenly she realized that there was nothing to fear in thinking about the past. Joe and Ricky could recount the tales of his temper and actually laugh about it. That should be her attitude as well.

The specter of her grandfather shrank to life-size in her mind. The relief was enormous.

Joe knelt down in front of the fence and started hammering on the lowest board. "Deep down he was a good guy," he said. "You just had to dig."

Darcy shrugged. She hadn't dug. What's more, she didn't think a person should have to dig to find the goodness in another person.

"Rick, hold this board in place, would you?" Joe asked.

Obviously delighted to be included in the repair, Ricky stepped forward and tried to lift the rail into place.

Darcy quickly bent down to assist him, and they held it together while Joe nailed. "This feels like a joke," she said. "How many people does it take to nail a board to a fence?"

"Three," Ricky answered seriously.

She and Joe laughed. "That's right," she said. "I wouldn't have thought you'd need so many of us."

"You need three people for a lot of things," Ricky said. "You need at least three people to play tag. And you need three people to make a family."

Joe stopped hammering. "We're a family, Rick. There are just two of us."

"We don't have a mother," Ricky said. "So we're not *really* a family."

That tugged at Darcy's heart. "I didn't have a father when I was growing up," she found herself saying to him. "But my mother and I were a family, just the two of us." Of course, that wasn't really true. And she'd felt the lack of a father for her entire life.

"What happened to your father?" Ricky asked.

"He died."

"Did you miss him?"

She nodded. "I missed him a lot."

"Didn't your mother get you a new one?"

Several, she thought cynically. "No, she couldn't find someone as nice as him."

"My mother was nice," Ricky said. Then he brightened and said, "You're nice too."

"Hold it steady over there," Joe said, and Darcy realized she'd let the board slip.

She took a shuddering breath. "You're nice too, Ricky."

The banging hammer suddenly became very loud.

"Scoot over, kid," Joe said after a moment, moving to nail the middle to a cross board. Ricky stepped out of the way and Darcy found herself shoulder to shoulder with Joe. "Come here often?" he joked softly.

A shiver ran down her arm. "Every ten years or so."

"I thought you looked familiar."

She looked down, feeling heat tint her cheeks pink. "Ricky, you want to hold this up now?" she asked, making room for Ricky between herself and Joe.

"Yeah!" Oblivious to the tension, he wedged himself between them.

Darcy stood up and wiped her hands on her jeans. "It looks like you don't need me here anymore. I think I'll go back to the house and help Anthea finish packing."

Joe gave a quick nod. "They're leaving tomorrow, huh?"

"First thing in the morning."

"I want to say good-bye again," Ricky said.

Darcy felt a stab of sadness for him, and for herself, that the Coxes were leaving.

"You've said good-bye to them four times this afternoon already," Joe said.

"But they're *leaving*," Ricky wailed.

"Tell you what," Darcy said, stooping beside him. "You help your dad fix the fence, and then, if it's okay with him, I'll come get you and take you to say good-bye to Anthea and Hank one more time after dinner."

Ricky looked at Joe. "Okay?"

"I'll take him up to the house," Joe said, sounding a little impatient. "You don't have to come get him."

She stepped back. "Okay, then." She smiled at Ricky, hoping he couldn't see the disappointment behind her smile. "I'll see you later."

Chapter Six

"I think we're paying too much for these day workers," Darcy said the next morning in Joe's breakfast room. "If we had guys staying here for pay and board, we'd save money in the long run."

"Except that there isn't enough usable living space anymore," Joe said.

"But how much could it cost to fix it up?"

"Plenty." The word sat between them like a giant slab of unmovable concrete.

"You know, Joe, I get the feeling that you're trying to make me feel like an outsider," Darcy said testily.

"You did that yourself," he said replied. "You're *still* doing it."

Before she could answer, Ricky came pounding in, shoes untied, his coat hanging off one arm. "Dad, I'm still hungry!"

Joe glanced at the clock. "The bus is going to be here in five minutes. Here." He reached into the kitchen drawer. "Have a piece of gum."

"Joe Tyler!" Darcy looked at him in horror. "You're going to send that child off to school with nothing in his stomach except...gum juice?"

"Darcy, I think I—"

"Good lord, I don't know how the two of you have survived all this time. You're lucky social services hasn't come out to investigate you."

"Darcy—"

She shook her head and clicked her tongue against her teeth. "Do you even have any healthy food here?"

"*Darcy,* not that it's any of your business, but he's already—"

She gave him a pointed look. "We'll talk about this later." She went to the refrigerator and looked inside. "What do you want, Ricky? Eggs? Bacon?"

"I had that."

"What?" She peeked over the refrigerator door at him. "When?"

"That's what I had for breakfast."

She tried not to look at Joe, whose gaze she could now feel burning on her cheek. "When?"

"When I got up." He slid his other arm into his jacket and stopped in front of Joe, extending a shoe for him to tie.

Joe tied Ricky's shoes, then glanced back at Darcy with his eyebrows raised. "I've been in your kitchen, you know. I wouldn't exactly call those chocolate diet drinks you have healthy food."

"They are, too, they have one-third of a day's supply of every vitamin you can think of. Plus the milk you add."

He gave a derisive laugh. "They're made of sawdust and sugar, nothing else. Besides—" he raked his eyes over her figure in a raw appraisal "—if anything, you could stand to gain a few pounds."

Try the forty I gained when my husband ran off with all my money, she wanted to say. *It took months to work that off.* Instead she said, "I'm not five. What I eat doesn't have anything to do with this."

"Neither does what Ricky eats." He patted his son on the shoulder and said, "You better get out there, son, or you'll miss the bus."

"Can I go by myself?" Ricky asked, beaming. "I'll stay where you can see me, and stop right where the bus driver can see me."

"Sure, go on." Joe laughed as Ricky gathered his backpack and lunch and ran out the door.

"I'm sorry, Joe, I was out of line," she admitted when Ricky had gone. "You do seem to be doing a pretty good job with him."

"Gee, thanks." Clearly he thought she'd been condescending.

She sighed. "You must miss Anthea, though."

"She was great with him," Joe agreed. "But we'll get by." His voice still held an edge.

Darcy flushed. "I didn't mean to offend you. I was only thinking of how Anthea was always so good at doing those little motherly things, like cooking hot lunches and stuff."

"You thinking of filling that role now?" he challenged.

Her face grew warm, but there was nothing she could say. She'd made a fool of herself, and she had the feeling it wouldn't be the last time. "I was only thinking it's too bad Anthea had to leave."

"And so it is. But she's gone."

"Why are you so cold?"

"Look who's talking."

"And what is that supposed to mean?" she flared.

"Ten years ago, you left here and never looked back. You can't imagine how that hurt...your grandfather. And the Coxes," he added quickly. The look in his eyes hardened and didn't waver. "Now you waltz back in when it's too late, and you can't get used to the fact that things have changed and that you can't just wave a magic wand and make them like they used to be."

Darcy's spine stiffened. "What business is *any* of that of yours?" she demanded. "Why are *you* so bent out of shape about my relationship with my grandfather and the Coxes, for crying out loud? It's got nothing to do with you!"

"No, I guess it doesn't," he said coolly. "I guess it never really did."

"That's for sure." She stared him down. He was so clearly over whatever tender feelings he'd once had for her that she wasn't going to give him an inkling of what she'd suffered over their separation.

He stared right back at her. "But I'll tell you one thing, I'm not going to spend the next two months being a whipping boy for your ex-husband."

"What?" How did Brandon come into this? She hadn't even discussed him with Joe, nor did she plan to.

"You obviously don't trust men. What'd he do? Cheat on you?"

"None of your business."

"It is if you're going to make me hang for it."

"Funny, he said almost the same thing about you."

"Me? What have I got to do with anything?"

She winced inwardly. If he had ever cared for her the way that she'd cared for him, he never would have asked such a thing. He would know. "Nothing. I'm just saying

I don't think you've exactly been the picture of loyalty, fidelity and honesty.''

''Oh, but I have.''

She gave a bitter laugh. ''Right. I remember.''

''You remember what?''

She gave him a piercing look. ''I remember just how loyal and faithful and honest you are.''

The look he returned was equally searing. ''I thought you didn't remember anything about our past.''

She took a breath and counted to ten. She couldn't let him get to her this way, and she sure couldn't let him know he did. ''Just because we had a meaningless relationship a hundred years ago doesn't mean you know me or have any right to comment on how I conduct myself.'' Even as she said the cruel words, she hated herself for the pretense, but once again pride wouldn't let her show Joe how vulnerable she'd been...and still was.

''Ditto, sweetheart.'' He walked to the cabinet and took out a battered coffee tin.

''This is all business.''

He opened the coffee tin and scooped some of the black grains into the top of an old percolator. ''Suits me fine.''

''So, sticking to business, what about how much we're paying those men?''

''They're not being paid what they're worth as it is.''

''Can we do without a few of them?''

He set the percolator on the stove and turned the burner on. ''No.'' He faced her, and the phrase ''tall, dark and dangerous'' came unbidden to mind. She felt her heart hammering wildly out of control and hoped he couldn't guess at the turmoil beneath her brittle facade.

She felt the humiliation freeze on her face. ''Would you care to elaborate?''

He did. He went in to great detail about how much work needed to be done, how much livestock needed attention, how much land needed work and how many men there were doing all of that. By the time he finished, she could see it was a pretty grim picture.

"Why are you so worried?" he asked. "Your grandfather left money for the ranch to keep going these two months."

"And then what?"

"What do you mean 'and then what'? Then we sell."

"What if no one buys?"

Several beats of silence pounded between them. "Someone will buy."

"Who?"

"I don't know. Someone. This is great land. Someone out there is bound to see the possibilities."

"I don't know. After all my grandfather couldn't make a real go of it. Look at it—the place is falling apart around us."

Joe poured two cups of coffee. "With all due respect for the dead, your grandfather was behind the times. He stuck to the old ways of doing things, and when the old ways became obsolete, so did the ranch."

"What could he have done?"

Joe shrugged his broad shoulders. "Lots of things. I talked to him over and over again about getting rid of the cattle and specializing in the horses—maybe quarter horses or thoroughbreds—but he was determined to do things the way he always had, even though beef consumption was way down."

"You're saying the T.L. didn't *have* to fall to ruin?"

"It absolutely didn't."

Darcy cocked her head. "Wait a minute, wait a minute. Do you have a pen and some paper?"

"Why?"

"So we can write this stuff down." She took the small pad and pen he handed her. "Let's write down our options. First, keeping the ranch and making it profitable."

"Wait a minute, that's not really an option."

"Why not? You just said it was."

"It was once. It isn't anymore."

"Why not?"

He heaved a breath. "The forty-thousand-dollar tax bill that's due, for one thing."

"I'd forgotten about that," she said in dismay, then wrote *tax bill* in the Cons column. Afterwards, she paused thoughtfully. "I have an idea. What if we sold off part of the property and used the money to pay the bills and get things running?"

"Can't be done," Joe explained. "The only land that would be valuable to anyone on its own would be the four- or five-hundred acres bordering Lyndon Keller's property, and he's refused for years to grant an easement."

"What does that mean?"

"It means that you can't sell the property because Keller won't let anyone have access to it via his property."

"Oh." She frowned. "You're sure he won't agree?"

"Your grandfather tried for years, but Keller has steadfastly refused. That's the only reason Ken sold half the cattle off five years ago. He didn't have any other options for raising money."

Darcy nodded and wrote *easement* in the Cons column under the tax bill. She looked at the paper, then at Joe. "Can we get another mortgage?"

"Did you read anything you signed?"

Her face grew hot. She sensed he was condemning her as the rich girl she used to be, careless about money because there was always more to be had. If he only knew how things had changed for her since those days! "Get to the point."

"Okay, the point is that the ranch is already mortgaged to a degree where I personally wouldn't be able to take the financial risk of a second mortgage." He studied her for a moment. "Did you have any interest in buying me out at the end of the term?"

"Me?" She pointed to herself. "No way. I told you, I have a job to go to in California. This place is the past for me, and it's going to stay that way."

He shrugged. "I wasn't sure that was definite."

"Oh, it's definite all right. I don't know how I'm going to spend two weeks in this boring little town, much less two months." She realized she probably sounded haughty and snobbish, but that was better than letting him know she was broke.

He put his hands up in surrender. "Okay, okay. I was only asking."

She raised her eyebrows. "No chance of you sticking around, either?" She doodled idly on the paper. "I mean, of buying me out?"

He gave a laugh and turned back to the stove. "Nope. Too rich for my blood. Though I would have liked to try breeding quarter horses here." He heaved a sigh. "But I have other commitments."

Darcy looked back at the paper. "So what it all comes down to is that keeping the ranch really isn't an option at all."

"That's about the size of it."

She tore the paper from the pad and crumpled it up. "Then that answers that."

"How do you like it?"

"I think it stinks."

He raised a cup. "Your coffee—how do you like your coffee?"

"Oh. Black."

He glanced dubiously at the cup, then handed it to her with half a smile lifting the corner of his mouth. Recalling the intensity of all her old feelings for him, she had to catch her breath.

"You're in luck," he said, handing her the mug.

As she took it, their fingers brushed against each other in the exchange. Her heart began to flutter wildly. "Thanks," she said, setting the cup down so he couldn't see the way her hand trembled.

"I think we should sell off the rest of the cattle right away," he said. "Then the horses. We've got a few foals here that should bring in some good cash."

"Okay." She took a sip of the coffee. It was strong and so bitter that her first instinct was to spit it back out, but she'd already made enough of a fool of herself for one day. She forced herself to swallow.

"I never claimed it would be *good* coffee." He smiled, and she remembered how many times she'd pictured that pirate smile in her dreams. Not that those old fantasies meant anything. There was no better fantasy man than one who was well and truly out of reach, and until recently Darcy had believed Joe was safely in her past.

"I suppose when you've wined and dined all over Europe, this tastes like poison," he concluded.

She grinned. "I think even to someone who's wined and dined all over Peoria this would taste like poison."

He laughed and she felt a little more at ease. If only her fingers would stop itching to ruffle his hair.

"You were saying we should sell the livestock," she went on.

"Yeah. The contract only said we couldn't sell the land for two months. We may as well get moving on this, so when our time's up we can move on."

Move on. Sell the place that had felt more like home to Darcy than anywhere else. She felt a flash of anger at her grandfather for having put it within her grasp but making it impossible to hold because of Joe. Grandfather knew— she felt sure he knew—that Brandon had run off with all her money, and that she'd never be able to buy Joe out.

He also knew that any personal dealings between herself and Joe would be difficult.

She couldn't understand what he'd been thinking when he set the conditions. She didn't understand any of it.

Joe looked at the clock on the wall. "Hey, I've gotta go. It's career day at Ricky's school, and I'm supposed to talk about being a 'cowboy.'" He gave a self-effacing laugh.

Once again, Darcy felt a twinge in her heart at the unexpected tenderness of Joe Tyler. Years ago she'd been drawn to his wildness, the part of him that seemed dangerous and decidedly undomestic. Now she was touched by the way he took care of his child.

"Look," Joe said, "I've got to go into Boulder later today. I'll see what I can do this afternoon about unloading some of the livestock."

"Great." She hoped her voice didn't sound as flat to him as it did to her.

"I'll let you know what I find out. Maybe we'll talk in the morning. Are you free?"

"No, my social calendar is pretty full," she said teasingly. At his answering grin, she relented. "Yes, I'm free."

"Good. I'll see you tomorrow, then."

She stood and followed him to the door, standing just outside it as he walked away. "See you then," she said softly, wondering at the intense longing she suddenly felt, and at the wild hope that it would someday be fulfilled.

The next morning they went to Tastee Maisy's Diner in town. Joe seemed perfectly at home in the loud, bright, stainless-steel-utensil atmosphere, but Darcy was on edge the entire time.

Unfortunately, when she was nervous she tended to babble.

"...I mean, why not spell *tasty* right? What's with these places?"

Joe leaned back in his seat and regarded Darcy with what looked like pity. "It's just a gimmick. Get over it."

She felt her face warm. "There's nothing to get over, I was only wondering why it is that certain types of places always have to pick a cute spelling over a correct one. This could have real sociological significance."

"I think it's even more sociologically significant that you haven't taken your jacket off or put your purse down in the fifteen minutes that we've been here," he drawled, his dark eyes staring. "Why are you so uncomfortable around me?"

"Who said I was uncomfortable?" Darcy asked, pulling her jacket closer around her.

"It's been obvious since the minute you saw me."

She tried to give a laugh. "That's pretty vain of you, Joe."

"Maybe." He shrugged. "Maybe not."

She took a sip of the tepid water in front of her. "What does that mean?"

"It means it's obvious you have a problem with me, and you've had it since before you found out your grandfather divided the ranch the way he did. Now, considering the fact that the last time you saw me was...well, given the circumstances of that last meeting, it has to be something to do with that."

She couldn't let him open that subject, couldn't let him see how vulnerable she remained, even after all this time. Better for him to think her callous than for her to acknowledge the power he held over her emotions. "Joe, that was ages ago. We were just kids then. How could I still have feelings about it now? That's just so ridiculous—"

"Okay." He splayed his arms in surrender. "I shouldn't have said it."

"I mean, I have a life, you know. I've done a lot of other things over the past ten years—"

"My mistake."

"It's not like I've been sitting around pining over you." She straightened her shoulders. "How pathetic would *that* be?"

"Enough!"

His face was like a thundercloud, his eyes hard and glittering. "Have I offended you?"

He shrugged, but the gesture seemed more forced than casual. "Not at all. I'm just trying to get to the point here."

The waitress interrupted to set a cup of steaming coffee in front of him. Joe gave her a dazzling smile of thanks, and Darcy guessed it wouldn't be long before the brassy-haired waitress was slipping him free slices of homemade apple pie.

Turning to Darcy, the waitress asked, "Would you like to order now, ma'am?"

"No, thank you, I'm fine." The waitress walked away, and Darcy looked at Joe. "All right, back to the point. What'd you find out in Boulder?"

He took a sip of the coffee and set it down with an appreciative smack of the lips. "Good stuff, Darcy. You should give it a try. It's nothing like mine."

"No thanks. What did you find out in Boulder?" she pressed.

"I found out that a lot of people are having trouble raising cattle."

"Oh, no."

"Yup. At the most, we could get half of what we talked about yesterday. It's hardly profitable."

Darcy did some quick figuring. "Except that if we keep them, we've got to keep that much more hired help."

"Or else you'd have to dig in and do some of the work yourself," he challenged.

She flared defensively. "I didn't say I wasn't willing to work, Joe. The problem is, I work better with my mind than with my hands."

"I remember otherwise."

Her breath caught in her throat, and a current of electricity shot down the core of her body.

"You did a heck of a lot of work on and around the barn." His devilish smile told her he knew exactly what she'd thought he meant. "You know, that fence hasn't been painted since you did it."

She cleared her throat. "Let's sell. It may not be profitable, but it will at least make our lives easier."

"You got it."

"What about afterwards?" Darcy asked suddenly.

"Afterwards?"

"After the two months are up. Are we going to sell it ourselves, or hire a real estate agent, or what?"

"We'll have to use an agent because I can't hang around to make the sale. Having a third person do that would probably be the most equitable solution anyway."

"*Neither* of us wants to hang around after that," she said pointedly.

He nodded slowly. "This must be a pretty sleepy place for a woman like you."

She shrugged. Was he remembering their old fantasy of settling down together on a ranch, communing with nature and each other? She wasn't going to let him think that fantasy still held any sway over her, especially since he'd clearly renounced it years ago.

The waitress reappeared with a plate of steaming scrambled eggs and enormous golden pancakes smothered in fluffy butter, with spicy-scented sausages on the side.

Darcy's stomach growled.

The woman set the tempting plate before Joe and poured him another cup of coffee. She gave a seductive smile. "Who's your friend, Joe?"

It figured she already knew his name, Darcy thought.

"This is Darcy Beckett, Ken Beckett's granddaughter." He gestured toward Darcy, but the waitress didn't avert her gaze.

"She moving in?"

"Yes," Darcy said. "*She* is."

Now the heavily made-up eyes flicked toward her.

"Welcome to Holt." She returned her attention to Joe. "And how's your boy?"

"Real well, thanks."

"He's cute as a button, that one. Gonna be a real heart-breaker someday, just like his daddy."

"Helene!" a heavyset woman behind the counter called. Darcy guessed that was Maisy. "Table four's waiting."

"Excuse me," Helene said to Joe. She walked away without a second glance at Darcy.

Darcy turned to Joe. "So what's waiting for you in Oklahoma?"

"You look hungry. Here." Joe moved his plate to Darcy's side of the table. "Have some of this."

Her stomach leapt. "No, really—"

"Look, I'm not sure what happens to your half of the ranch if you die of starvation, but I'm not willing to take the chance." His eyes held hers for a moment. "Go on, eat." Without waiting for a response, he signaled Helene for another plate.

Darcy persisted. "So what about Oklahoma?"

"I've got a job at a ranch out there. They've been waiting for me for a long time."

"So when do you have to leave?"

"Don't worry, I'll be here as long as I have to be."

"I'm glad to hear it." She knew she couldn't ask for more than that. Really, she shouldn't care. She *didn't* care. "So, how did you get this job?" she asked casually.

"From an old friend."

He didn't elaborate as she'd hoped he would. "Good for you," she said. "Hmm."

Helene reappeared with another plate and set it down on the table. For a moment Darcy and Joe ate in silence. Joe was the first to speak.

"So are we straight on what we're doing? Selling the cattle and horses?"

"Yes, I guess so." She hesitated. "What old friend? Why are you being so mysterious about this?"

Joe blew air into his cheeks, then leaned forward. "Here it is. I had no idea that Ken was going to leave me anything in his will when I made these plans and now I have no choice about leaving. But the fact remains that I have to give my son a home, and the sooner the better. So that's what I'm going to do. There's nothing mysterious about it."

Darcy swallowed the urge to ask why he had to leave the area to give Ricky a home. "Okay, but when are you leaving? Do you have a solid date?"

He hesitated as if considering whether she had a right to know *anything* about him. Finally he looked her dead in the eye and said, "I have to be gone no later than January fifth."

She tried to catch her breath. "What's your hurry—are you wanted by the FBI or something?"

He gave a dry laugh. "I don't think even *that* could get me out of it. But don't worry about it, Darcy. You don't need me here while the place is on the market. When you find a buyer, I'll come back and sign the papers. Meanwhile, you can live here free and clear. It works for everyone."

The plan did make sense, but the way he was suggesting it—or maybe just the fact that *he* was suggesting it—made her balk. "I don't know if that's right. After all, I have to leave too."

"So what's to stop you?" He glanced at her plate. "You just about finished?" Suddenly he sounded as if he didn't have a care in the world. He took a large bite of his pancake, then a sip of coffee.

She looked at her clean plate. "Yeah. Just about."

He signaled to Helene for the check. It was clear he wanted this meeting over.

Helene lay the check in the middle of the table.

"All right." He picked up the check, examined it, then pulled a bill out of his wallet and set it on the table.

"How much do I owe you?" Darcy asked, making a movement toward her purse and praying she could find enough quarters inside to cover her bill.

"Forget it," Joe said, waving her off.

"I can't let you—"

"Come on, Darce." His blue gaze was so penetrating she felt as if he could see right through her. "Call it the date we never had."

Her face grew warm. "We had dates."

"I wouldn't call meeting in the barn after dark a 'date.'"

"You didn't seem to mind at the time."

He hesitated, then said, "Best times of my life. But I thought you deserved better. I wanted to take you out like regular people. You know—dinner, movies." He looked as if he were going to say something else, but he shrugged and took a sip of his coffee instead.

Her chest felt tight. She couldn't believe he still had this effect on her. "It was the best we could do at the time."

"At the time," he agreed. "My timing has always been lousy."

She didn't answer. She couldn't think of anything to say.

After a few minutes, Joe spoke again. "How did your husband let you go?"

Darcy started, then thought she must have misheard him. "What?"

"I was just wondering what happened to your marriage." He gave a casual lift of his shoulders. "You never said."

"You seemed to have your own theories."

He looked down and fidgeted with his cup. "What I said before, well, I was just mad—"

"Don't worry about it."

"—for all I know, you dumped him. That wouldn't surprise me. I never could quite see you married anyway."

Darcy gave him a harsh look. Every time she thought she might have misjudged him, he came up with something that proved how little he thought of her. "Just what does *that* mean?"

"Nothing bad," he said quickly. "You just don't seem to stay in one place for too long."

He shrugged. "Some people like to move around, I guess."

Darcy shook her head but said nothing. He was so far off the mark. She couldn't make him understand even if she tried, which she wasn't about to do.

Apparently that was fine with him. With a final gulp of his coffee, he stood up and said, "Let's get going." He walked toward the door.

Darcy picked up her purse and followed him out, feeling as if there was more to what *he* was going through than he was saying. "Joe, wait a minute."

He stopped outside the door and turned back to face her. "Yeah?"

"Is there something you're not telling me about your move to Oklahoma?"

He put his hands on her shoulders and looked deep into

her eyes. "Darcy, there's a *lot* I'm not telling you." He gave a light squeeze then pulled back. There was a somberness in his eyes that she hadn't seen before. "But none of it concerns you so, like I said, don't worry about it."

"Don't worry about it," she repeated dumbly.

"Right." He turned and walked away. "You'll get your money," he said, then added quietly, "Everyone will get their money."

Chapter Seven

"When did you used to know the lady that moved into Mr. Beckett's house?" Ricky asked his father that afternoon as Joe was driving him to a friend's house.

"Who, Darcy?" Joe kept his eyes fastened to the road. In the back of his mind, he remembered a newspaper article that stressed the importance of not reading too much into a child's questions. "I knew her a long time ago."

"You liked her a whole lot, didn't you?"

Joe cleared his throat, startled at his young son's perceptiveness. He wished he could remember what else that article had said. "Once."

"Dontcha like her anymore?"

"I like her just fine."

"I like her, too."

Joe gave a nod. "Good." End of subject. Whew! That was close. Joe was about to take a deep, relaxing breath when Ricky spoke again.

"I want her to be my new mom."

Suddenly Joe's hands felt slick on the steering wheel. "You want *what?*" He tightened his grip and frantically searched his mind for some clue as to how to deal with this conversation.

"I said I want her to be my new mom."

Joe sucked air in through his teeth. He had hoped, maybe foolishly, that Ricky had gotten over this desperation for a mother. Over the past few holidays, such as Mother's Day and Valentine's Day, he'd made cards for a mother who didn't exist. Not Maura, Joe realized a little sadly. She had died before Ricky had had much awareness of her role in his life. But once he'd entered nursery school and all the other kids had mothers to make cards and pictures for, Ricky had done it, too.

Joe's chest ached as he remembered the first time he'd found one of the pieces of folded construction paper, colored carefully in crayon, with the words *Hapy Valentins Day Mommy.* Joe had recognized the big, sloppy handwriting as Ricky's, even though he wanted to believe that it was someone else's, that the card had gotten in Ricky's backpack by mistake.

He looked at his son's profile and felt a lump lodge in his throat. Somehow Ricky had decided that Darcy was the perfect maternal surrogate. Where the heck had that come from? Joe had dated one or two other women over the years and Ricky hadn't said he particularly wanted *them* for the job.

Joe forced himself to take a breath. He was totally unprepared to even think about this, much less talk about it. New mom, new wife. Was there anything Darcy was less suited for, other than, say, army life? "Who said we were in the market for a new mom?"

Ricky sank down in the seat and turned to look toward the window. "Everyone else has a mommy."

"Darcy is not the mom type," Joe said, more to himself than to Ricky. "She's not the wife type either."

Ricky didn't ask what Joe meant, but Joe found himself talking as though he had. "Maybe a guy could go out with a girl like Darcy some, dinner here and there, but he'd have to be a Rockerfeller to marry her."

Ricky turned back to his father with troubled eyes. "You couldn't marry a lady like Darcy?"

Joe pressed his lips together and shook his head. "No way."
He increased the pressure on the accelerator. The sooner they reached their destination, the sooner this conversation would end. "Definitely not."

"Why not?"

"Why not?" Joe echoed. "Well, because she doesn't like to do the same sorts of things we do." He knew Ricky would ask what he meant by that, so he tried to think of examples that would make sense. "She wouldn't like to eat at Peppy's Pizza Palace. She wouldn't like the milk shakes at the Dairy Queen."

"What would she like?"

"Champagne," Joe answered without hesitation.

"What's that?"

"It's like liquid gold." At Ricky's puzzled look, Joe elaborated. "It's a very, very expensive drink. Every mouthful costs about as much as—" he tried to think "—a box of crayons." Then, in case there was any doubt, he added, "That's a lot of crayons."

"Oh." There was a long silence. "But what if she drank something else? *Then* could she be my new mom?"

Joe drew to a halt at a stoplight and reached over to

muss Ricky's hair. "It's not about what she drinks or what we eat, Ricky." He looked into his son's clear blue eyes. "Darcy likes to move around a lot. She wouldn't be happy staying in one place like this for very long. We wouldn't want to keep her here if she wasn't happy, would we?"

"Couldn't we move with her?"

The light turned green and Joe pressed the accelerator. "We need a home, bud. We need to settle down. We need to have a place to really call *home*." The center line sped by as Joe drove out of town. "Darcy doesn't fit into that picture."

"So you don't want her," Ricky said with rising anxiety. "And you don't care what I want."

"I do care what you want—"

"No you don't! You don't care at all. You don't even care that I don't have a mommy!"

Something twisted in the pit of Joe's stomach. Could he go so far as to say he didn't want Darcy? Somehow the words didn't come to him. "I care a lot, son, but there are other things we have to think about right now."

Ricky sniffled loudly, and Joe knew it meant his son didn't agree.

Maybe someday he would understand.

And when he did, maybe he could explain it to Joe.

His conversation with Ricky came back to Joe the next morning when he met with Darcy to go through the main house and decide what they had to fix up in order to sell. They'd already agreed on the few improvements that needed to be made in the barns and paddocks. They'd also agreed that the tenant house, where Joe and Ricky were living, needed very little beyond a coat of paint.

The main house was the last frontier for them and the

single most important part of the formula. If they could get it into good shape, it might entice a buyer into purchasing the whole property.

Joe watched Darcy walk up the stairs of the main house in front of him. They were supposed to be assessing the house's needs, but right now all Joe could think about were his own. That subtle sway of her hips probably wasn't deliberate, but his body reacted as though it were. All these years had gone by and he still responded to Darcy like a hormone-laden teenager. If there was any doubt in his mind about the power of the chemistry between them before, it was gone now.

Joe sighed. Lusting after Darcy was one complication he did not need right now. He had a ranch to run and sell, and, most important, a son to raise.

"I don't want to spend a lot of money, but I also don't think we should cut corners," Darcy was saying. "The ranch deserves the best."

"Never mind us, huh?"

She stopped at the front door and turned to face him. Except that she wasn't exactly facing him, since she was two steps up, leaving him to face her chest. "You have to take me seriously, Joe."

He groaned. "Believe me, Darcy, I take you completely seriously. And I love this place as much as you do, but the fact is, I can't afford to spend a fortune fixing it up only to leave the state."

"Don't you care who buys it?" she asked, then scoffed and said, "No, I guess you just want to get this over with so you can move on, get out of here."

"You know, the more you talk, the more I think you should be staying here yourself."

"Me?" She shook her head and opened the door. "No way."

"It seems to mean an awful lot to you."

Her eyes flitted downward before she looked at him and said, "It doesn't mean anything. I just think it's a good idea to fix it up as well as we can. Ten dollars' worth of paint may translate into ten thousand dollars' worth of selling price."

He studied her in silence for a moment. Suddenly it seemed very clear to him that Darcy really didn't want to sell. But what choice did she have?

They started with the library. Joe figured this room would be easy. "Okay, we'll need to fix the shelves and the moldings around the windows, but otherwise I think this room is fine." He wrote that down in the small notebook he'd brought and slipped his pen into the spiral binding. "Next room?"

Darcy curled her fingers around the large clipboard she had picked up off the hall table on the way in. "You mean, after we strip and repolish the floor, and add a couple of brass library ladders on runners."

"Actually that isn't what I meant."

"We also need to replace the glass in the windows."

He couldn't believe his ears. "What's wrong with the glass in the windows?"

"It's chipping a little around the edges. It's only a matter of time before the windows are completely cracked."

"It's a quarter of an inch thick. A little chipping doesn't matter. It adds character. Besides," he reminded her, "you're not going to be here."

A pained expression crossed her face. "You want the ranch to sell, don't you?"

"Yeah—"

She put her hands on her hips. "If you're so anxious to get out of Holt—"

"I'm not the only one who's anxious to get out," Joe argued. "What about you and your destiny in San Diego?"

She didn't answer.

He took a deep breath and tried to remember his objectives. "Look, all we have to do is make the place presentable and let the real-estate agent do the rest. You have to let go, Darcy."

She clenched her jaw and stared hotly at him. "It's none of your business whether I let go or not—"

"That's true."

"—but, for your information, I *have* let go. I already told you, several times, why I want to make improvements."

He shrugged. "It doesn't sound to me like you're interested in the economics of resale. I think you want the place for yourself."

"*If* that were true—and it's not—what would you suggest I do? Rob a bank to buy you out?"

He smiled patiently. "How about getting a loan?"

She muttered something under her breath.

"What?"

She looked at him with eyes blazing. "I said, I can't get a loan."

He scoffed. "What do you mean you can't get a loan? Hell, your family founded the Holt Savings and Loan. Maybe you're just used to having things handed to you instead of having to pay for them."

Darcy took a short breath, then another. When she finally spoke, it was through her teeth. "Okay, you asked, so here it is. Along with my youth, my money and my dignity, my husband took my good credit rating. There isn't a bank in the United States that would loan me a penny, much less the kind of money it would take to buy you out.'' Her eyes grew misty but her voice maintained a steely tone. ''So I'd really appreciate it if you would drop this subject and not pick it up again.''

She didn't wait for him to answer. Instead, she turned on her heel and walked out of the room, leaving Joe to feel like the biggest jerk in Colorado.

She wasn't looking forward to seeing him again, and somehow managed to avoid it until the next afternoon, when they met in the work shed where they had put the paint and brushes.

''Listen,'' Joe said when she came in. He was mixing a can of paint, but he stopped and looked at her. ''About yesterday...I shouldn't have said anything. It's none of my business how you feel about the ranch.''

''Forget it,'' Darcy said quickly. She hadn't wanted to think about it yesterday and she didn't want to think about it today. It was uncomfortable enough to have to face her fragmented past herself, much less justify her feelings about it to Joe.

''Darcy, don't you like the ranch?'' Ricky asked as he came around the corner of the shed. He sat down, surrounding himself with matchbox cars, perfectly happy to play while his father worked on the paint.

''Hey, sweetie,'' Darcy said, stepping over to him. ''Of course I like the ranch.''

''Me too. I wanna stay.''

''Rick, you know that's impossible,'' Joe said. ''We can't stay. We're going to a new home.''

Darcy winced. *New home.* How many times had she heard those words? Too many times to count. How many times had they been correct? Not once. No place had ever felt like home.

Except for the T.L. Ranch, that is.

But, Darcy reminded herself, that feeling was just a psychological trick. *A happy person is happy anywhere and a miserable person will be miserable anywhere,* her mother used to say. It was strange that Darcy had always been a happy person at the ranch and a miserable person elsewhere.

Coincidence?

"*This* is home," Ricky protested.

"We're a family," Joe said. "Wherever we're together is home."

"We're not a family." Ricky's face grew pale, with angry red splotches on his cheeks. "We don't have a mother." He glanced at Darcy, then back at Joe.

Joe's expression became stern. "Families come in all shapes and sizes. You and me are a family and we get along just fine without a mother."

"*Everyone* has a mother," Ricky wailed. "I want one!"

"I don't have a mother," Darcy heard herself saying.

"You don't?" Ricky sniffed.

"No, she lives very far away and I haven't seen her in years."

"Big surprise," Joe muttered.

She flashed him a look and he raised his hands in surrender.

"Do you miss her?" Ricky asked Darcy.

"Yes." Darcy thought about it. "I think I know exactly how you feel. But your daddy is right. You have him and that makes you guys a family. And that's very lucky."

"Who makes *you* a family?" Ricky asked.

She gave a half smile and shook her head. "I'm my own family right now."

"That's sad."

It didn't feel good to have the pity of a preschooler. "No, I'm fine living the way I am." Even to her, the words sounded hollow. "I made a choice to live this way and I'm happy with it."

"Oh." Ricky looked unconvinced. Then, with a slight shrug, he rammed one car into the other. "Oh, they ran into each other."

"That seems to be happening a lot around here," Darcy said. She turned to Joe. "I got some new moldings for the library window this morning. Should we split the bill now or put it all into a file and take it out after the sale, or what?"

Joe straightened and frowned slightly. "How much was it?"

"I got a good deal," she assured him a little nervously. "We had to get the good stuff."

"No," Joe said. "We didn't. *You* did. And I'm not going to let you run me into the poor house while you try and make this place into the home you've always wanted. We're leaving. You're leaving, I'm leaving, we don't need to go nuts fixing the place up."

"I'm not trying to make it into the home I've always wanted!"

"Yes, you are."

"According to *you*…"

"No, according to you. I vaguely recall talking about this a long time ago. You've always wanted to fix up that library."

"I have not!" Her voice, though loud, lacked conviction. It was coming back to her, too—a conversation with Joe about what she'd do if the T.L. Ranch was hers.

"You remember," he said confidently, returning to mixing the paint. "Think about it. You're spending all this money to make this place into your ideal home."

She gave a broad shrug, hoping to appear nonchalant. "Think what you like—"

"Daddy said you drink gold," Ricky piped from the corner. "Is that true?"

Darcy looked from Ricky to Joe, then back again. "Your daddy said I drink *gold?*"

"Champagne," Joe muttered, giving Ricky a warning look. "It made sense in context."

Ricky nodded and went on. "He said that's why you can't be in our family."

Darcy shot a look at Joe. "In your family?"

"Yeah, that's what I was trying to say before, but you guys started fighting about the library. I asked Daddy if you could be my new—"

"O-kay, Ricky, I think that's enough." Joe stood up and headed toward the boy. "Let's move you out into the yard now. I think you need some sun."

Darcy put out a hand to stop him. "No, I think he's just fine where he is." She shot a glance at Joe. "Really, it's okay." She looked back at Ricky. An unfamiliar pang resounded in her heart. "I'm not related to you guys, that's why I'm not part of your family."

"But wouldn't you be if—"

"Aw, man, we don't have time for this now." Joe raked his hand through his hair and shifted his weight from one foot to the other.

"But, Dad, you said she—"

"Come on, Ricky, you can come help." In three long

strides, Joe was at his son's side, helping toss the toy cars back into their container.

"You said I what?" Darcy asked Joe. Her eyes flicked over to Ricky. "What else did he say?"

"That you wouldn't be interested in making a family with us. He said you're not *that* sort of lady. But *I* thought you were." He puffed up his chest proudly.

"Well, you're a very clever boy," Darcy said. "I'm sure your dad meant well." She gave Joe a look that belied the words. "*Whatever* he said."

Before Joe could stop him, Ricky said, "He said that you get around." He wrinkled his nose. "I'm not sure what that means."

From five feet away, Joe heard her quick intake of breath.

"Now, wait, I never said that." He flashed a look at Ricky. "You've got that wrong, I didn't say that." He looked back at Darcy and repeated, "I didn't say that."

Ricky nodded vigorously. "Uh-huh, you said that Darcy gets around, so she isn't the kind of lady that men marry."

Joe's face grew flushed. "No, I swear I didn't say that. You're misquoting me, Ricky."

The boy looked at him quizzically. "Huh?"

It was all Joe could do to force himself to face Darcy. She was glaring with every bit as much heat as he expected. "Darce, he's got things confused."

"It all sounds very clear to me."

Joe tried to laugh. "That's the irony of it. He's gotten it wrong but it makes sense."

She raised her eyebrows.

"Not that it's correct," he amended quickly. "Because of course it isn't."

She folded her arms in front of her and shifted her

weight from one foot to the other, glaring at Joe all the while.

"It's really very funny," he said lamely, moving toward her.

"Oh, I'm sure it is," she answered without a hint of amusement.

He guided her out the door, into the bright sunshine of the yard. "What I actually said was that you're not the kind of girl a guy like *me* marries." He splayed his arms, as if that made everything clear and all right.

"Ah, I see."

"I knew you would." So why did she still look so angry? In fact, why did she suddenly look angrier than she had before? "What's wrong, then?"

"Nothing," she replied curtly. "Perhaps later I can take Ricky to dinner and tell him about guys like you."

"I told you I didn't say all that stuff. I thought you understood."

"I'm afraid I do."

"Then—"

"Let's just stick to business, okay? We don't have a personal relationship. Let's just keep it that way."

"Okay." He threw up his hands. "Business."

"So why were you talking about me that way?"

Joe took a long breath. "Ricky really likes you—"

"I'm so glad to know that someone around here does."

Joe glanced at Ricky, then drew Darcy around the corner to talk privately. "Yeah, well, God knows you've done your best to prevent it."

Darcy raised her chin and Joe noticed a slight tremble in her lower lip. "If you're having trouble with me, it's not my fault. Maybe you should examine yourself more closely to find out why you can't deal with me."

"I can't deal with you because..." He fumbled for the words, looking from her eyes to that trembling lip and back again. Why couldn't he deal with her? Because his feelings for her had never died? Nah.

"It's because you're impossible," he contended hotly.

"Oh, well, since you're going to be so specific." She threw her hands up. "You're pretty impossible yourself."

He looked into her clear blue eyes and felt the old catch in his throat. This time words failed him completely. He'd spent so much time thinking of her over the years, thinking of her with anger at times but also thinking of her with so much tenderness it made his heart ache. The way it was aching now....

With a groan, he pulled her into his arms and kissed her.

Chapter Eight

Darcy parted her lips automatically, deepening the kiss. Joe thrust his tongue into her mouth and explored, delicately playing against her tongue. Pleasure coursed through her, sending liquid fire through her veins.

She curled her arms around Joe's powerful back and held on tightly. Only for a moment, she thought, savoring his taste and the feel of his arms around her. Just one moment can't hurt anything, she told herself. Every small movement was eerily familiar, as though the years of remembering had not altered the truth but only faded it slightly. Because this feeling was more powerful, more delicious, than anything she could recall.

"I remember this," Joe murmured against her mouth, clearly finding the experience similar to hers.

"Me too," she said softly. She trailed her hands slowly up his back and across his shoulder blades. He was stronger now than when she'd met him, more solid. A man, not a boy. She loved the feel of his muscles rippling under his cotton shirt. He was still the perfect height for her, she thought vaguely as she curled her hands around his shoulders.

Joe splayed his hands against her lower back, pressing her against him further. She felt his belt buckle nudging against her abdomen, but the sensation was not unpleasant. She'd missed this closeness. She'd been thinking about it, somewhere in the back of her mind, ever since she first laid eyes on Joe again.

He ran his tongue across her lower lip, then kissed her cheek, her chin, and, when she tipped her head back, her throat. This was paradise. If Brandon had made her feel like this, even once, maybe they could have worked it out.

She stiffened, suddenly remembering young Ricky's words. *Darcy gets around, so she isn't the kind of lady that men marry.* Joe kissed her mouth and for a moment she sank into it, allowing Ricky's words to fade, but then she remembered Joe's own words of explanation. *What I actually said was that you're not the kind of girl a guy like me marries.*

She pulled back.

"What's wrong?" Joe murmured in her ear.

She withdrew farther. "You can't just have your way with me and think I'll forget what you said."

He stepped back completely and looked at her with raised eyebrows. "What does that mean? And, by the way, that—" he pointed to where they'd just been standing "—was not 'having my way with you.'"

"Oh, no, for 'girls like me' I suppose that was just a warmup." She sounded childish and she knew it, but his words had stung her to the quick.

"What are you talking about?"

"I'm talking about what Ricky said."

Understanding came into his eyes. "I told you his version wasn't exactly accurate."

"Maybe, but it didn't come out of the blue, either."

Joe let out a long breath and rubbed his jaw distractedly. "Look, Ricky's really cottoned to you. I knew that, but when he suddenly started asking if you could be his new mom, I was taken by surprise."

Darcy nodded. "Go on."

He gave a half shrug. "That's pretty much it. I tried to explain to him, in terms he could understand, why that wasn't going to happen. It's not like I could get into all the subtle man-woman things with him."

"Ah." She nodded again. "So instead, you simply told him I wasn't the sort of girl men marry, and then let him draw his own conclusions."

"He's not even capable of drawing the conclusion you jumped to."

"So you told him—"

"I told him," Joe said softly, "that you lived a different sort of life, moving around a lot, and that you couldn't be happy with a guy like *me,* who could settle in one place for the rest of my life. You want excitement, I want a home."

"He also told me he liked you a lot," said Ricky, peering out the door.

Joe jumped. "Ricky get back in there with your toys!"

Darcy went over and put a protective arm around Ricky's shoulder. "It's not his fault you chose to confide in him." Her heart was beating double time. He'd told his son he liked her a lot.

Ricky looked up at Darcy with wide eyes. "He doesn't mean anything, he's just loud sometimes," he said in an unconcerned way. "But I didn't get it exactly right. He said he likes you a *whole* lot."

"Ricky—" Joe began.

"You *told* me I had to get things right or don't repeat them!"

He groaned and threw his hands in the air. "That's it, I'm leaving. You two can work this out yourselves." He strode off into the sun, his footsteps making dull thuds on the ground until he was out of sight.

"Women," Joe muttered to himself as he crossed the lawn in long strides. "No," he corrected, "not women. *Darcy.* Darcy Damned Beckett." He kicked a large rock in his path. "Everything was fine, I had a plan—maybe not a great plan but a plan—and then Darcy came along and *wham*—" he kicked another rock "—everything blows up."

He got to the small barn where they kept the broodmares and shoved the door open. Several of the horses threw their heads up in surprise. "I thought I'd never see her again," Joe went on, speaking aloud. He stopped at the stall of a very pregnant gray mare named Ladybug. "I would have been fine if I'd never seen her again," he said to the mare.

Ladybug didn't respond.

"No, I would have been *great* if I'd never seen her again." He opened the stall door and went in, running a careful hand along the horse's neck and across her withers. "Not that I never thought about seeing her again. I mean, I *thought* of it, once in a while. Years ago." He exhaled loudly. "Somehow I just never thought it would be like this. Under circumstances like *these.*" He sighed. "I never thought it could be so...so...*electric.* I mean, what we had was ages ago."

He touched a hand to Ladybug's swollen belly, and the horse nickered. He patted her withers soothingly. "I guess you just never know when your past is going to come back and haunt you, do you?"

The horse turned and nuzzled his arm. He ran his hand across her neck. "What the hell was Ken thinking? Why would he specify that we had to live here *together?* I would have thought that was the last thing in the world he wanted." He stopped and gave a wry chuckle. "I guess it *was* the last thing that he wanted."

He ran his hand across the mare's underbelly, feeling for the foal's position. "She really does look great, though. Just—" he sucked the air through his teeth "—great." He straightened up and shook his head. "*Man.* Why does she have to look so good?"

He let himself out of the stall and walked down to the feed room, still shaking his head and continuing his conversation with himself. "And the way she is with Ricky...the look she gets in her eye. Of course, she knows nothing about kids, but it's really something to see her try. It's like..." He stopped and considered. "It's like she really cares—for now."

He opened a bin and dumped several scoops of sweet feed into a black rubber bucket for Ladybug. He carried it back to her stall, thinking about the look Darcy had whenever she talked to Ricky. As if she really wanted to understand him, to help him. As if she genuinely cared about the little boy. "But, of course, she'd get tired of that *real* fast," he said, flipping the rusty latch on the stall door. He reached in and hooked the bucket next to the water trough. "It's not like she could ever commit to living a quiet life out here in the country. She'd probably go crazy if she had to spend six months without a glimpse of the Caribbean.''

He went back to the feed room and got another bucket of feed. ''Not that I would hate to get a glimpse of the Caribbean myself,'' he admitted, walking to another stall and unlatching the door. ''But there's Ricky to consider now. He needs a home, a normal kid's life. School terms, a packed lunch box, bedtime stories.'' He hooked up the bucket and closed the stall door. ''That's not Darcy's kind of life.'' He laughed at the very idea. ''She'd be miserable.''

He looked over the schedule to see if any of the other horses were due to be fed. As he ran his finger down the paper, he noticed the ingrained dirt, and the black under his fingernails that remained no matter how hard he scrubbed. It was the perfect illustration of how different he and Darcy were. ''Why am I even thinking about this?'' he asked himself, walking down the main aisle to see what else needed to be done. ''We've only got a tiny bit of history—and no future at all.''

None of the other mares needed attention, so he walked out of the barn, closing the door a little more gently this time. ''And as for the present—hell, we're just barely together on this.''

Suddenly he thought of Rosanna, waiting impatiently for him in Oklahoma. Rosanna, insisting that it was the best thing for Ricky that he be with a mother figure such as herself.

''No future at all,'' he repeated softly. ''Even if we wanted one.''

''So your dad said he likes me a lot, huh?'' Darcy prompted Ricky with a wry smile. They were headed for the kitchen in the main house. After Joe's abrupt exit, they'd both decided they could do with a snack.

Ricky nodded. "I like you, too. Why don't you want to stay with us?"

Darcy walked across the kitchen and opened the refrigerator. "First of all, *I* didn't say I didn't want to stay here with you." She pulled out the celery.

"So you *are* going to stay?"

She set the celery on the counter and went to the pantry. "I didn't say that, either." She took the peanut butter out and placed it next to the celery. "There's someplace else I have to go when we're finished fixing up this house, but it's not because I don't like you or don't want to stay with you." She took the top off the peanut butter and dipped in a stalk of celery.

Ricky nodded, taking the peanut-butter-tipped celery she handed him. "So it's Dad that you don't like? Is that why you're going away?"

She was beginning to see how this had happened to Joe. "No," she said, mustering patience. "I *do* like your dad. I like him a lot." The last part sounded a little wistful, even to her own ears, so she added, "But it has nothing to do with whether I stay here or move to California."

"Why *are* you moving to California?"

"Because it's time for me to get my very own home."

"But isn't *this* your home?"

She hesitated. She wanted to answer, but the words didn't come easily. "This was the closest thing I ever had to a home—but, no, it's not my home. Not anymore."

Ricky crunched down on the celery. "I don't understand grown-ups at all."

This, Darcy decided, was a mistake Joe had made. He had let Ricky misunderstand everything, then had walked away without explaining it to him. "What is it, exactly, that you don't understand?" she asked, ushering Ricky over to the table where they sat down with the peanut butter jar between them.

"Dad likes you and you like him and we all live here. Why does everyone have to move away?" He screwed up his brow and looked at Darcy. "Is it because you don't like kids?"

"Oh, no, no, no," she reassured, laying a hand on top of his. "It's nothing like that. I haven't had much experience with kids, but I told you I like you an awful lot. However, just because people like each other doesn't mean that they should live together."

She searched for an example in her mind. "You like your teacher at school, don't you?"

"Miss Marion?"

Darcy brightened. This was working. "Yes, Miss Marion," she said knowledgeably.

"Nah. She's mean."

Darcy deflated. "Oh."

"But I like Mrs. Wilkins, from recess," he added helpfully.

"Good. Okay, you like Mrs. Wilkins but you don't want to live at her house, do you?"

He narrowed his eyes, considering. "Would my dad be able to come?"

Frustration pounded in Darcy's chest. Maybe she wasn't doing such a bang-up job of this after all. "Look, Ricky, I'm just going to tell this to you straight. A man and a woman need to really *really* like each other, in a very *special* way, in order to live together and be parents together."

"You mean in a kissing sort of way?"

"Exactly." Relief coursed through her. He understood.

"You and Dad just kissed. I saw."

Her face burned. Now what? She had to dig her way out of this before an inaccurate report of it got back to Joe. "No, they have to do it a *lot*," she said lamely.

"Oh," he replied.

She waited with bated breath for the next misunderstanding to follow that deceptively simple response. But he remained silent for a few moments.

"So I'm glad we got that settled," she said tentatively, her statement curling into a question at the end.

Ricky wrinkled his nose. "But you would marry dad, if you liked him in that really special way and kissed a lot?"

It seemed to her that it was as close to accurate as she was going to get with Ricky. "Well, yes, I suppose so." She wondered at the wisdom of leaving it at that and decided it would be safer to elaborate. "If two people like each other, in that particular way, and they both feel the same, there's no reason why they shouldn't get married if they want to."

"And if they kiss more."

She sighed. "Okay."

He dipped the last stub of his celery into the peanut butter. "I think I understand now."

"I'm so glad." She looked at the remaining three stalks of celery and, desperate to change the subject, said, "I wonder if I should have saved that for Thanksgiving..." She shrugged to herself. "What am I saying? It wouldn't last that long."

"When's Thanksgiving?" Ricky asked.

She looked at the date on her watch. "In two weeks." She glanced at Ricky. "Do you and your dad have plans?"

He shook his head. "Don't think so. We don't have big

holidays like other kids' families. Dad calls Thanksgiving 'Turkey Day' and that's all that's different—we eat turkey.''

"For me, too,'' she admitted. For her, Thanksgiving had pretty much always been just another day, but she'd regretted that fact every year. When she was married she'd tried to make holidays special, but it hadn't worked out. It wasn't something she liked to think about. She returned her attention to the child in front of her. "But for you guys it should be a special holiday.''

He nodded, seeming to understand. "It's more for boys?''

"No,'' she said, trying not to laugh, "it's for families.''

"Not as easy as it looks, is it?'' Joe's smooth masculine voice came from the doorway behind her. There was more than a hint of amusement in it. Still, the relief she felt at his return surprised her.

But she couldn't let him know that. "We're not having any problem,'' she said, turning to face him. "Except that your son doesn't seem to think Thanksgiving is about anything but eating turkey.''

Joe's cool blue eyes didn't flicker. "We don't make too big a deal about that kind of thing.''

"Maybe you should.''

He raised an eyebrow. "Why?''

She lowered her voice, hoping Ricky wasn't paying attention. "Because if you don't, it might affect him later.''

Joe waved the notion away. "Eating turkey is how we celebrate.''

"At Denny's?''

"Sometimes.'' He smiled then, and pointed a finger at her. "I see what's going on here.''

"What?''

"You're the one who wants to have a Thanksgiving dinner and you're trying to rope us into it with you."

She laughed, but it sounded a little shaky. Suddenly she felt naked. "Don't be ridiculous."

He was still shaking his head. "This isn't really about Ricky at all. This is all part of your whole 'this is home but I'm in denial' thing."

"I don't have that…that *thing*. And I certainly wouldn't use a little boy as an excuse." Oh, God, was she? she wondered.

Joe's grin broadened. "Pretty clever, Miss Beckett." He clicked his tongue against his teeth.

She felt the heat creep up into her cheeks. "*Ms.* Beckett. And that's not what I'm doing at all."

He leaned against the door frame. "So what time do you want us to come?"

"I didn't say *I* was going to do it. I said I thought you should be having a Thanksgiving dinner with your son. Now, since you've said you already have big plans to go to a restaurant—"

"Should we bring anything?"

"No—"

"Not even some wine?"

"I'm not making Thanksgiving dinner for you two."

She felt a tug on the back of her shirt. "Why not?" Ricky asked her. In just two minutes of arguing with Joe, she'd completely forgotten the boy was in the room. "Is it because you don't have enough celery?" He indicated the three stalks on the table.

"No, that's enough, I guess." She realized what she was saying, and added, "If you guys want to borrow it to make your turkey stuffing, you're welcome to it."

"Turkey stuffing?" Ricky repeated.

"Stove Top," Joe told him and the boy nodded.

Darcy groaned.

"We're not big on cooking in our house," Joe explained, looking somewhat pathetic. On purpose, Darcy suspected.

She couldn't help smiling. "Obviously." She looked at Ricky then. His hope-filled eyes made her heart contract with sympathy.

What would it hurt to have Thanksgiving with them? Maybe it would do Ricky some good. Maybe it would even help inspire Joe to make more of holidays for his son in the future. Darcy sighed. "All right, I'll do it."

Two pairs of eyes looked at her with equally genuine warmth, but it was Joe's gaze that really set her heart thumping.

"Perhaps this will start a new Tyler tradition," she said pointedly. "If you help me cook, you may just learn how to do it for yourself next year."

"I've seen you cook," Joe said. "And I'd say it isn't half as much fun doing it alone."

She swallowed. Were they talking about cooking? "I won't be there to do it for you next year."

"We'll do this one year at a time then." He watched her for a moment, then jerked his thumb in the direction of the front door. "I'd better get back out to the barn. There's a broodmare out there who could drop it any second."

"Drop it?" Darcy asked, raising an eyebrow.

"Ladybug is going to have a baby," Ricky explained.

"Ah." Darcy nodded, and extended her arm. "By all means, then, go."

Joe held her gaze. "Can I see you later?"

Her eyes trailed down to his lips, then snapped back.

She hoped that he hadn't noticed. What was she thinking? "Why?" she asked casually.

He looked startled. "We have some financial things to discuss." He glanced at his son. "Maybe after Ricky goes to bed?"

"Tonight?"

His mouth cocked into a half smile. "You've got other plans?"

She narrowed her eyes at him. "What time?"

He shrugged. "Eight-fifteen, eight-thirty."

"Okay."

He started to leave, then stopped and turned back. "Can you come down to our place? I hate to leave him alone in case he wakes up."

"Sure." She looked from father to son and noticed, for the first time, the similarity in the shape of the eyes and the straight brow. She felt a brief pang of longing, wondering what it would feel like if Ricky were her own son and Joe were her— "Fine, I'll be there," she said, interrupting her thoughts before they got out of hand.

Joe hesitated, almost as if he knew what she'd been thinking. Then he put a hand on Ricky's shoulder and guided him out of the kitchen. "Let's go, bud." He stopped outside the doorway and turned back. "See you tonight," he said to Darcy.

She swallowed and tried to find her voice. "Yup."

Darcy stayed still, watching for a long time after they were gone, seeing the image of the father and son, side by side. There was affection in their proximity, even in the space between them. It was a sort of manly protectiveness that seemed to say, "You're a man, too, and even though you don't need me to be, I'm here for you."

Her heart ached as she thought again of how a mother

must feel when she looks at her husband and her son. She imagined the pride, the delicate thread of hope and fear for the growing child. She didn't *want* to imagine it—after all, what was the point? She wasn't the type of person who could be a mother, manage a home, take care of a family. She didn't have the temperament for it at all.

A mother, she told herself, should be the sort of person who had all the answers to life's problems, big and small. A person who was calm in the face of crisis and would distribute comfort and wisdom over cups of tea at the kitchen table. A mother should be smart and jolly. A mother should know how deep a cut had to be to get stitches, or how high a fever had to be before the doctor was called.

A mother couldn't be restricted by tons of emotional baggage. She couldn't lie in bed at night, her mind and pulse racing with fear of an unknown future. Most of all, a mother should *not* be a person who had made a mess of her own life and who so often felt pangs of wanting a mother herself to take care of everything for *her.*

By the same token, a wife should also know how to handle things in the home and family. When she'd been married before, Darcy had often felt her own limitations. Granted, it wasn't everyone who needed to know how to post bond when her husband was jailed in a gambling bust. Still, Darcy realized that a wiser person would have taken care of business and then gotten out of there. Instead, she'd relied on an expensive lawyer to take care of things. And she had proceeded to flounder in a marriage that didn't feel right, or even good, because she'd believed one of her own mother's biggest flaws was that she'd given up on her marriages too easily.

She thought of Joe and Ricky. It was odd how they

brought these thoughts to her mind. Perhaps it was because it was "safe" to think of them that way. After all, in a few short weeks they'd be moving miles and miles away from her, to the life they'd already planned.

And she would be...where? San Diego, she supposed, but the idea didn't have the charm it had held when she'd started driving west. Still, she knew that staying here wasn't an option.

She glanced in the direction Joe and Ricky had gone, and sighed.

Chapter Nine

It wasn't the first Thanksgiving dinner Darcy had ever cooked, but she was determined that it would be the best.

The first thing she needed to do was find a cookbook. She knew more or less how to cook a turkey and vegetables, but she wanted to make a great meal and she didn't know how to do that. When she had made Thanksgiving dinner for her former husband, Brandon pronounced it "okay" and got a burger from the local burger joint after dinner. He had to go out anyway, he explained, none too patiently. His team had won the game. He had to collect.

She pulled a book off the kitchen pantry shelf. It had a faded beige cover, which might once have been white, with the words Regional Cookbook stamped on it in flat black lettering. It didn't look all that inspired but it was the only thing she found after fifteen minutes of searching.

Idly she leafed through the pages, delighted to see that there was writing in the margins—lots of writing in a round handwriting she didn't recognize. "Use parsnips instead of carrots," one note said. "Add a pinch of baking soda to the boiling water," another commanded. Some sort of cookie called Winham Wopsies had a cheerful little note that "the children love these."

As she leafed through the pages, Darcy was warmed by the homey notes and additions to recipes. One or two were crossed out with "don't bother" or "horrible" next to them. Darcy smiled. This was a person who didn't mince words. She turned back to the first page and looked at the name, written in the same, careful round cursive: *Lillian Bryson* and then, apparently added later in a darker ink, *Beckett*. Lillian Bryson Beckett, Darcy's grandmother.

An old photograph of a couple and two children was pasted beneath the name. Darcy looked closely and vaguely recognized her grandfather's features—the wide eyes, prominent cheekbones and pointed chin—in the face of the man.

Tears sprang to Darcy's eyes. Why she would have an attack of melancholy now, she didn't know. After all, she'd never met her grandmother. She didn't even know anything about her really, except the recently revealed fact that her grandfather had named their home the True Love Ranch in her honor.

The thought of her grandfather brought more tears to her eyes. This time she knew why. For weeks she'd been trying to avoid thinking about all the time she could have had with him but didn't. Now, standing in his dilapidated kitchen, looking at the recipes for meals her grandparents must have shared many years ago, it hit her full force.

Yes, her grandfather had been gruff, but she'd always known he loved her. Those summers here made for some of the sweetest memories of her life. She should have dwelled on that rather than on his "betrayal" all those years.

She looked back at the picture with a sigh. Once upon a time her family must have been close. What had happened?

The question was pointless. She knew what had happened. The Beckett family had a habit of being so full of pride that they let the things most precious to them slip away. She was a prime example. Granted, it had been unfair of her grandfather to react to her marriage the way he did, no matter how right he was about her husband. But if she had acted like a grown-up about it right off, maybe they wouldn't have lost each other.

She sighed. Coulda, shoulda, woulda—who could tell what might have been? Her time would be better spent thinking about the problems in her life that could benefit from practical solutions. Like the ranch. Like Joe Tyler.

She dropped the picture and it slipped to the floor. When she bent to pick it up, she saw that the faces were no longer those of her grandmother and grandfather, but were unmistakably of Joe and herself. She gasped and dropped the picture again, face down. For a few moments, she sat, heart pounding, staring at the back of the photo. The faces had been clear, but perhaps the most eerie thing about it was that they looked somehow *right*. They looked happy together. She swallowed, then swallowed again.

It had to have been her imagination, she told herself. Photos don't change like that except on old TV sitcoms about genies and witches. A voice drifted through her mind, saying it was the magic of the True Love Ranch.

She tried to scoff. "It's the magic of too little sleep," she said aloud. "That's all."

She looked back at the picture on the floor and hesitated

before picking it up. When she turned it over again, it was once again of her grandmother and grandfather. She touched the old textured surface and immediately felt like a fool. It had been a trick of her imagination.

She let out a long breath. She wished she could allow herself to want Joe, or at least to have the luxury of a few daydreams. But she didn't think she could take another Joe Tyler heartbreak, and if she were to actually allow herself to *desire* him, that would surely be what she'd suffer.

Deep inside her heart—so deep she could barely see it— she *did* think about him, though. She did wonder what it would feel like to make a home with him, to be his wife, to be a mother to Ricky. After all, he'd been her first love. He was a large part of the reason the ranch had always meant a great deal to her, even in memory. Once upon a time she would have thought that the True Love Ranch held some magic. Not now, though.

Having convinced herself that she'd merely imagined the photo incident, she returned her thoughts to the Thanksgiving dinner she was planning. She knew she'd need turkey, so she flipped through the index and found the roasting instructions. There was also a recipe for chestnut dressing. She took out a pen and started to make a list of ingredients.

By the time she was finished, she had a list two pages long and she'd marked six pages in the cookbook. She leaned back and smiled to herself.

This year it *was* going to be different.

"Every real-estate agent I talked to wants an exclusive contract with us," Darcy told Joe later that night. They were again sitting at the table of his small, comfortable kitchen. Two cups of convenience-store coffee steamed on the table between them. "The woman I particularly liked won't work without an exclusive. But I have a lot of confidence in her. I think she'd do well for us. A real go-getter."

"Hmm." He tossed a couple of tiny envelopes across the table to her. "Cream and sugar?"

She smiled. "What, no plastic stirrer?"

He stood up and went to the counter. After a moment of digging in a white paper bag, he tossed a tiny red straw to her. "We've got it all." He smiled easily and leaned against the counter. Darcy felt he was looking down on her, literally.

"All right, so what about the real-estate agent?" she asked. "Do we sign an exclusive with someone?"

He smacked his lips together and shook his head. "I don't know, Darcy, it smacks of commitment to me."

"Commitment?"

He nodded. "Signing legal papers together, committing to one person, all that sort of thing."

She raised her chin. "I didn't ask you to marry me."

He laughed. "No." He pushed off the counter and walked toward her, standing behind her with a presence as strong and impenetrable as steel. "No, you didn't."

"I promise I don't have any such designs on you." She hoped he didn't hear the catch in her voice as he laid his hands on her shoulders.

He kneaded her muscles gently, withering her defenses. "Ah, but would you keep your promise?"

She narrowed her eyes. "Are we talking business?"

He hesitated, then, with his lips so close to her ear that she could feel the warmth of his breath, replied, "Of course."

"It certainly doesn't seem that way." She tried to

straighten her shoulders but she was weak beneath his touch.

"Well, if this isn't business, I suppose you'd call it pleasure."

She tipped her head back and looked up into his eyes. "Then you have a lot to learn about pleasure."

He grinned. "Really? You used to think otherwise."

She drew in a quick breath. "I don't remember. And these days, it's none of my business anyway. Your personal life, I mean."

"It could be," he said, bending close and speaking into her ear.

"It shouldn't be," she said weakly.

"Why not?"

She cleared her throat. "We already have way too much *business* together. What about the real-estate agent? What do I tell her?"

"Tell her 'okay.' I've always been a one-woman man." He pressed his lips against her neck.

She tried to pull away but it was a futile attempt. The only way she could break the contact would be to stand up and she was...she was *resting* just now. And she'd be damned if she'd let Joe force her out of it.

Yeah, that was it.

"I'd call this unbusinesslike," she said to him. "Would you please stop...manipulating me and go sit down."

"Do you really want me to?" He bent down behind her and spoke quietly into her hair.

"I think so." But she leaned back against him.

"I don't." He trailed his tongue up to her earlobe, then nipped lightly.

She let her head fall back completely, opening herself to his kisses. "I do," she said feebly.

"Yes? You sure?" He ran his hands down her arms and then clasped the back of the chair.

As long as she stuck to her guns, she couldn't be blamed for anything that might transpire. "Mmm, hmm." Before she knew what was happening, he'd tipped her chair back and closed his mouth over hers.

The kiss was lingering but gentle. For long seconds neither of them moved, then Joe pulled back and pushed her chair forward. The jolt knocked her senses back into her. She stood up, pushed the chair out of the way and faced him. "That kind of thing has got to stop."

He took one step to close the gap between them.

She fought the urge to take a step toward him.

"I never could resist you," he said huskily, reaching to take her hands.

She didn't stop him. "I hardly think I'm irresistible."

Holding her gaze with his own, he lifted her hands slowly, running his fingertips across her wrists. "There are those who would disagree."

"Are there?"

He moved his wrists until their hands were flat against each other, palm to palm. "Did you ever think about the communication of touching?"

"No."

"Sometimes it's better than trying to talk." He looked at their hands and she followed his gaze. "Because you can say more." She glanced at him and saw that he'd turned to look at her face. Their eyes locked. "And you can't lie with a touch."

She studied his strong hand around her slender one; his still-tanned-from-summer skin against her pale skin; his strength enveloping her delicacy. She tightened her grasp.

He ran his thumb across hers, back and forth in a mesmerizing rhythm.

There hadn't been a moment in her marriage that was half as intimate as this. She closed her eyes.

She sensed his movement and didn't back away. When his warm lips touched hers, she responded immediately, parting her lips and thrusting her tongue toward his. They released their hands and wrapped their arms around each other. Joe flattened his palms against her upper back and pressed her closer, moving the pressure slowly down to her lower back.

She sank into him willingly, holding him as close as she could. Satisfaction filled her like warm cocoa. He was delicious, as he'd always been, in her memory and in her imagination. She drank him in, knowing that it should be the last time, that before long they were going to have to stop flirting with romance and go their separate ways.

Joe tugged at her T-shirt, loosening it from her jeans. When his hands touched her skin, she gasped and arched toward him. He took his time moving along her back, pausing every once in a while to concentrate on her mouth, bringing such sweet pleasure to her that she thought she'd faint. He unhooked her bra with a single flick of his fingers, then moved his hands across her ribs to her breasts.

"I want you," he murmured against her mouth, cupping her breasts with his hands. "I've never wanted anyone like I want you."

"Joe, we..." She tried to object, but the more he fondled her, the less strength she had for objections.

There was no one here to stop them this time. No thundering voice to demand an explanation, no 'punishment' for their attraction. They could go into his room right now and make love until the sun rose and there would be no horrible consequences.

She touched her fingertips to his belt buckle, then hesitated. There were consequences to everything. If she followed this impulse, she would almost certainly end up heartbroken and alone. Joe and Ricky were a family, and they already had plans to move away after New Year's. Those weren't plans that could possibly include her. A year from now, she and Joe would be worlds apart. They might as well be moving to different planets.

"Stop." She pulled back and looked into Joe's surprised eyes. "We have to stop."

"Why?" There was more than a little frustration in his voice.

"Because it can't go anywhere." She shrugged. "Beyond the bedroom, that is."

"Where do you want it to go?" he asked softly.

"Nowhere," she said defensively, tucking her shirt back in. "There *is* nowhere for it to go. That's why we have to avoid this temptation. We're too old to indulge in plain physical attraction."

Darkness fell over his expression. "Right. It's not as if we could have any kind of future together."

"No. Of course not."

He walked away, stopped at the counter and turned back. "You're on your way back to the big city. *Some* big city."

"Right."

"So no more personal stuff."

"Right." She thought for a moment. "Except Thanksgiving."

"Maybe that's not such a great idea after all," Joe remarked.

"But Ricky's counting on it. We can't let him down just because we don't have the good sense to resist the occasional physical temptation—which, by the way, undoubtedly comes from each of us being alone for so long."

Joe stared at her for a moment. "Nicely put."

She felt her face grow warm. "What did you want me to say? We can't keep our hands off each other?"

He looked at her for another long minute, then shook his head, combed his hand across his hair and walked across the kitchen. It was obvious that he felt rejected. "Did we get everything straightened out now?" he asked, all business. "I mean, about the realtor?"

She nodded. "I think so."

"Good. Is there anything else we *have* to talk about tonight?"

Her heart started to pound. She wanted to make it right somehow, to ease the tension that was building between them, but she didn't know what to say. "Well, no, I guess not."

He went to the door and opened it. "Fine, then. I'm going to check on the mare. You can let yourself out."

"Joe, wait." Something like panic made her nearly shout the words.

He stopped without turning back. "What?"

"What about Ricky?"

"He'll be fine. I'll only be gone a few minutes." He started to move.

"Joe."

He stopped again and she heard him suck the air in through his teeth. "Yup?"

"Are you mad?"

He sighed impatiently and turned to face her. "I'm not mad, Darcy. I just have things to do."

She stood up. "Okay. Go then."

He let go of the door and it banged shut. Darcy sat for a moment, watching him walk into the darkness, then decided to look in on Ricky before leaving.

There was a night-light plugged into the socket next to Ricky's bed. His unlined features were like smooth gold in the mellow light. Darcy sat down on the edge of the bed and touched his hair. "Good night, sweetheart," she said, gently running her finger across his soft cheek.

Ricky rolled over, hugging his stuffed rabbit closer to him. He mumbled something unintelligible.

"What did you say?" Darcy asked, hoping to sound like a voice in his dream and not wake him up.

He mumbled again, and rolled onto his back. This time she distinctly heard the word *Thanksgiving,* only it sounded like "Tanksgiving."

"You're looking forward to Thanksgiving, huh?" she whispered.

Still asleep, he smiled and nodded. She noticed his tiny fingers burrowing into the scrunchy stuffed animal.

She couldn't help imagining what it would be like to have Joe waiting for her in the other room as she tucked Ricky in and kissed him good-night. Another child entered her fantasy, too. A baby, sleeping in a crib in yet another room.

A family. A family with Joe.

She shook her head and blinked back tears. It was a silly fantasy: the remnants of her teenage crush. Joe would probably be mortified if he knew she was entertaining thoughts of a future with him.

"We'll have a wonderful Thanksgiving," she whispered in Ricky's ear, rising carefully so as not to wake him. "Don't you worry, we'll have a wonderful time."

Chapter Ten

They'd agreed to make Thanksgiving a working holiday and spend the morning together deciding who was going to do what in terms of the rest of the painting.

Unfortunately, they couldn't agree on what needed to be done, much less who was to do what.

"Forget it, then," Darcy said at last. "We'll just spit and polish and hope for the best. You're already halfway to Oklahoma anyhow. Let's just get this over with." She shook her head. "How much longer are we going to be trapped here together?"

"One month, two and a half weeks," he answered quickly.

She glanced at him, surprised. "You're counting?"

"You bet."

She sniffed, then threw her hands up and stood in one swift movement. "Why did he do this to us?"

Joe was bewildered by her outburst. "Why did who do what to us?"

She turned to him, eyes blazing. "Why did my grandfather leave this ranch to us, under such strict conditions? Did he intend it as a punishment?"

"No." Joe shook his head slowly and stood up to go to her. He placed a hand on her shoulder gently and guided her back to her seat. "I'll tell you what I think. I may or may not be right about this, but I think your grandfather was trying to make up for something he thought he did wrong."

"By putting us through this hell?"

"No, by giving us the opportunity to be together." Her eyes narrowed, so Joe quickly said, "Of course, we can both see how silly that is, but I think your grandfather had some preposterous idea that we were the big love of each other's lives." He tried to laugh. "Crazy old man."

Darcy frowned. "Yeah, crazy. So what gives you that idea?"

"Actually, he told me once. He said that he should have known better than to—as he put it—'stand in the way of young love.' Said he figured it was his fault that you married badly."

"Ah." She nodded. "So he punished *me* for what he thought was *his* fault. Sorry, Joe, I can't quite buy this."

"It's true."

For just a moment she wanted to believe it. Then common sense intruded. "Then why didn't he just say so? Why didn't he say he was wrong and he wanted to make it right?"

Joe shook his head gravely. "You know as well as I do. That wasn't his style." He hesitated, then said, "You know, he thought this place held some sort of, I don't know, enchantment or something for lovers."

She thought of the old photo, and how she'd seen her face and Joe's in it. "For himself and my grandmother?"

"I guess. He didn't talk much about that, except to say once that he missed her every day of his life."

"He actually *said* that to you?"

Joe nodded. "Once. When he'd been sick for a while. Maybe it was something he wanted passed along to you, who knows? Anyway, I think this will business was his way of matchmaking from beyond the grave."

Darcy gave a nervous laugh, unable to get the photo out of her mind. "Well, he was several years late and quite a few dollars short."

"Right." Joe heaved a breath.

"So since we're both going on our way soon—" she deliberately didn't say how long "—why don't you tell me why you're going to Oklahoma and why it's set in stone that you leave on January fifth."

"What's to tell?"

"I don't know, but every time we talk about it, you close up like a turtle going back into its shell."

He pointed a finger at her. "That's one of Anthea's expressions."

Her face colored. "I guess it must be in the air... But you're avoiding the question. Why do you have to go?"

"I owe my sister-in-law money," he said simply. "My wife borrowed it from her when she was ill and I couldn't be the monster who refused, so now..." He shrugged. "I owe her a lot of money and she's got a big ranch in Oklahoma that's in need of a foreman, so I'm working it off. Simple as that."

Darcy's face paled a little. "What if you paid her back? Then would you be able to get out of going?"

"Sure. But that's not going to happen. And even if it

did, I don't mind going. As she's pointed out time and again, it'll be good for Ricky to be part of a real family environment.''

Darcy nodded and looked pensive, but didn't speak.

"I don't like to talk about it," Joe finished.

"Sorry—"

"No, I— It's okay that you asked. I've thought of telling you a few times, but we always ended up talking about something else. Or arguing. What about you? What's in San Diego?"

"There's a scholarship program my father used to work on. Now his former partner's health is failing, so he offered to let me take it over."

"So what's it for, helping Ivy Leaguers find the right school?"

"Actually, it's a grant for underprivileged kids, so they can have the same opportunities as those Ivy Leaguers you're so disparaging of."

He immediately felt ashamed. He kept trying to cast Darcy as the spoiled, selfish rich girl, but every time he did, she proved him wrong. "I'm sorry. I didn't mean— That was rude of me, I'm sorry."

She gave him a long look, then said, "Forget it. I have to baste the turkey." She checked her watch. "It's just about time to start the vegetables, too." She looked at him with more kindness than she thought he deserved at that moment. "Why don't you come help?"

"Isn't this woman's work?" he teased, following her into the newly painted kitchen. Anything to bring their tone back to normal.

"Very funny." She handed him a five-pound bag of carrots and a potato peeler. "Here you go."

He set them by the sink and went to work while she

fluttered about, taking ingredients out of the refrigerator and pantry. They worked in silence for a few minutes, then Joe asked, "What are you making there? A pie?"

"You've got to have pumpkin pie on Thanksgiving," she said, pressing the cold pastry dough down with the heels of her hands. The dough was sticky, so she reached for the flour and sprinkled it across the counter. It puffed up onto her sweater. "Darn it," she said. "Where is that apron?" She looked around and found one on the back of the pantry door, hanging on a knob.

Joe laughed. "I've seen Anthea do that a hundred times."

"At least I'm in good company," Darcy said, slipping the apron on.

He remembered seeing her do that before. His heart moved into his throat as he walked over to her. "Need some help, ma'am?"

She turned to face him, her eyes wide. "Joe…"

He leaned against the counter, not making a move toward her even though he ached to. "You know, this is just how I used to picture you and me in the future. In a kitchen just like this, acting like a family."

"We're not a family," she said in a thin voice.

"Are we ever going to talk about that day?" he asked. "What day?"

"You know what day. The last day I saw you. The day we were in the kitchen, and you were making a pie, and your grandfather came in and ruined our lives. At least, he ruined my life that day."

She pressed her lips together. "That was a long time ago. I barely remember it."

"I remember it like it was yesterday." He took a step toward her. "You were standing there, trying to put your apron on, and I came in and put my arms around you like this.'' He demonstrated.

She trembled under his touch.

His hands weren't too steady, either. "And then I kissed you, like this.'' He lowered his mouth onto hers.

For a long moment, time seemed to stop. There was nothing but the tender kiss, just like the one that was interrupted so long ago. He moved his mouth over hers and she responded, timidly at first, then with more passion.

When they finally stopped, he held her close and whispered. "I've been wanting to finish that kiss for a long time.''

Her eyes were watery. "It was finished a long time ago.''

"No, it wasn't. I'm not sure it is yet.''

She swallowed and met his gaze for a long time. At last she said again, "I've got to baste the turkey.'' She hurried to open the oven and pulled the tray out with a pot holder.

"That's just like you—turn away when you're in a pinch.''

"You don't know me as well as you think you do, Joe Tyler.'' She basted the turkey and pushed the tray back in.

"You don't think so, huh?''

"No, I don't. Take what you just said about the scholarship.'' She took three sticks of butter out of the refrigerator and unwrapped them one by one, dropping the butter into a large saucepan on the stove. "You think I'm a spoiled rich girl.'' She gathered the butter wrappers into a ball and tossed them across the room into the trash can. "Admit it.''

"Okay, I admit I thought that.'' But he couldn't admit that he didn't think it anymore.

She looked at him aghast. "I expected you to deny it, at least a little."

He laughed at her confusion. "You think I'm such a stupid country bumpkin that that's all I can see in you?"

She hesitated. "So that's all you meant?"

"What do you think?"

"I'm not sure I want to know."

He shrugged and turned back to the carrots.

She took a few tentative steps toward him. "Okay, I want to know."

He didn't look at her. "You sure?"

Her footsteps stopped. "No."

He let the silence last a little longer than was comfortable, then turned to her revealing a smile. "Darcy, I think deep down you know how I feel about you."

A myriad of emotions crossed her features. "I'm not sure I do."

He shrugged and picked up the pile of peeled carrots. "Well, if you don't know," he said with a smile, dropping the wet carrots into her hands, "then there's probably no point in my telling you."

In the early afternoon, Darcy and Ricky decorated the dining room to make it festive, taping cardboard turkeys and pilgrims on the wall and making a centerpiece out of gourds and dried corn. Then Darcy sent Ricky out to play while she took a brief nap before returning to her preparations in the kitchen.

Dinner was on the table at five o'clock. Ricky came in from playing at four, just in time to put the marshmallows on top of the mashed sweet potatoes. If he had to have vegetables, that was the way to do it, with candy on top.

Darcy remembered that it had always been an enticement for her as well.

The three of them sat at the long, polished mahogany dining room table. Darcy had spent more time than Joe thought was worthwhile polishing the table, but now, in the glow of the candles and the dimmed chandelier, she was glad she'd done it.

She looked across at Joe, who had dressed for dinner. It was the first time she'd ever seen him 'all cleaned up,' and he looked delicious. The candlelight emphasized the fine bone structure of his face, which was usually masked by at least the shadow of a beard.

"This is great, Darcy," he said, taking a big bite of her sour cream mashed potatoes. He nodded appreciatively, mouth full.

"Thanks." She had to admit it had all turned out pretty well. It was the first time she'd ever made most of the recipes, but she'd followed the instructions carefully—including her grandmother's handwritten amendments—and everything had worked perfectly.

"My teacher says that Thanksgiving is when you go be with your family," Ricky said, peeling a browned marshmallow off his potatoes and popping it into his mouth. "Does that make us all a family?"

"It takes a lot more than eating a meal together to make a family," Darcy said.

"Not always," Joe said under his breath.

"Oh, yeah." A light came on in Ricky's eyes as he looked at Darcy. "You said you and Dad have to kiss more if you're going to be a family."

Darcy's face turned hot. "I didn't say—"

"But I saw you kissing each other."

Joe laughed, raising Darcy's hackles. "I think you've

got your facts mixed up again, son. If we were going to be a family, Darcy and I would have to get married and all that sort of thing.'' His gaze moved slyly to her. ''And that's not likely to happen, is it, Darce?''

''Not likely,'' she agreed, barely breathing.

His voice softened a little. ''We'd never be able to agree on where to live, for one thing.''

She shook her head. ''I can't see you moving to California.''

He tightened his lips. ''And I definitely can't see you moving to Oklahoma.''

She nodded her agreement. ''Of course, we're here now.'' She paused. ''This isn't so bad.''

''You don't think so?'' He raised his eyebrows knowingly.

''Do you?'' she asked quickly.

''Me? No, I don't think so.''

She lifted her wine glass thoughtfully. ''Of course, we both have other commitments after this one.''

''That's true.''

''Things we couldn't possibly get out of at this point.'' She raised her eyebrows in question.

''Probably not.''

''*Probably* not? Could you?'' she asked, taking a sip of the wine. It was important to sound casual. She only hoped he couldn't hear her pounding heart.

''Could *you?*'' he countered. ''I thought you were desperate to get out of this place.''

''Why is this about me? I thought you had already promised your services elsewhere, regardless of what happened here.''

Joe glanced at Ricky, who was concentrating on scooting his peas around the plate with a fork. He returned his steady blue gaze to Darcy. "Is something happening here?"

She swallowed. "What do you mean? With the house?"

"No."

"Are there any more sweet potatoes?" Ricky interrupted. His plate was already full of them, but he'd eaten the crusty baked marshmallow off.

Darcy found herself breathing a sigh of relief. The tension was getting awfully thick and she was terrified that she might say too much and make a fool of herself in front of Joe.

"You eat the ones you have first," Joe said, frowning slightly.

"You, too," Darcy said, pointing with her fork at his potatoes sans marshmallow.

Ricky laughed, but Joe gave Darcy a look that made her skin prickle. To change the subject, she asked the boy, "So, Ricky, are you going to see Santa Claus at the mall?" She shifted her glance to Joe. "I think he's going to be there starting tomorrow."

Joe looked bemused. "Well, I hadn't—"

"*Santa Claus* is going to be at the *mall*?" Ricky gasped. His eyes were open wide.

For a moment, Darcy was speechless. She'd thought surely Ricky had been to see a mall Santa before. She looked back at Joe.

"You just can't help but cause trouble, can you?" Joe said in a low voice, the smallest hint of a smile playing on his lips. "I can't take three hours off this year to drive all the way out there and wait in line." He lowered his voice still more. "I figured it wouldn't matter if he didn't know."

"Then I'll take him." The words flew out of her mouth

before she had a chance to think about them. What did she
know about taking a kid to see Santa? Then again, how
much did she need to know? You stand in line, send the
child up to tell the man what he wants for Christmas, then
take him home with a warm heart and a toy. How hard
could that be?

Joe looked pained. She knew she'd backed him into a
corner. He couldn't possibly refuse her offer now without
breaking Ricky's heart and looking like a heel at the same
time.

"Okay, then," he said slowly, looking from Ricky to
Darcy and back.

Before she could respond, Ricky let fly with a tremendous "Hurray! When can we go? Can we go tomorrow?"

Darcy thought about it. If there was one thing she knew,
it was malls. And the day after Thanksgiving was a crazy
day to go into one. "How about Sunday?" she suggested.
"That gives us two days to try and talk your dad into
going." She deliberately avoided meeting Joe's eyes.

"You volunteered," she heard him say. "This is your
party." Then to Ricky, "You can tell me all about it afterwards, how about that?"

"Sure." Ricky's enthusiasm was boundless. In a stage
whisper, he added, "And this time I'll try to remember
everything that Darcy says about you, just like you always
ask."

"Come on, come on." Darcy tightened her hands on
the steering wheel and prayed for the old car to make it at
least to the next exit. It shuddered and lurched. "Keep
going."

"What's the matter with the car?" Ricky was strapped
firmly in the passenger seat; he'd dressed himself for the

occasion. Darcy's heart did a flip when she looked at the little form in his slightly-too-small blue suit with a yellow summer cotton shirt. "Why's it making that noise?"

"Because it's a wretched old contraption that's been waiting for years to strand me on a road just like this." She looked at the narrow, winding country road before them. The engine was getting weaker and weaker, so when she saw a clearing ahead she decided it would be best to just admit the car was in trouble and pull over.

"What's 'rechid'?" Ricky asked.

Darcy looked at him, his eyes so wide and curious, and she laughed. "Wretched, in this case, means broken." She ruffled his hair, then reached for her purse on the floor in front of him. "With any luck at all, we're within a cell and at least my phone will work." She took her cellular phone out and pushed the power button, fully expecting the "no service" light to come on. Fortunately, it didn't. She dialed Joe's number, but the phone rang and rang. Finally, when she was about to hang up, he answered.

"Where the heck were you?" Darcy asked.

"Just fine, thanks for asking. How are you?" His voice hardened, and she knew he suddenly remembered she was out with Ricky. "Everything okay?"

"Yes, we're fine, but we're having some car trouble."

"What sort of trouble?"

"It's dead." She told him where they were and he said he'd leave right away. By her estimate he'd be there in about 20 minutes. She hung up the phone and slipped it back in her purse. "Well, it looks like your old dad's coming to see Santa with us after all."

Chapter Eleven

"I want the window seat!" Ricky cried, as Joe pulled up in his pickup truck.

"I think we'd all fit better with you in the middle," Darcy suggested.

"Nu-uh, I called the window!"

Joe gave Darcy a sober nod. "It's true, he called it first." He tried not to grin. "I heard him."

He caught the merest hint of a smile on her face before she said, "Okay, I call the window seat on the way home."

"What do you mean 'on the way home'?" Joe asked, climbing back into the driver's seat. "We're on the way home now."

Ricky looked crestfallen.

"Joe, we haven't seen Santa yet," Darcy said gently. "After all this—the car breaking down, waiting an hour for you to come—surely you don't expect Ricky to go home without having seen Santa."

He stifled a sharp objection. "Darcy, we've got nearly a hundred horses at the ranch that I'm taking care of single-handed. You can't seriously expect me to give up an hour to go to the mall."

"For one thing, you've hired several day guys to come in and work the horses, which they're undoubtedly doing right this minute, so stop your complaining. I think the horses can survive an afternoon without you."

"You'd better hope they can."

"And for another thing, I don't think it's *my* expectations that matter at the moment." With a tilt of her head she indicated Ricky.

Immediately Joe felt ashamed. It was true: he didn't have much time to waste, but he certainly didn't need to gripe about it in front of Ricky. Especially when the trip to see Santa meant so much to the boy. "No, you're right. What I meant was that we can't stay all that long."

Ricky brightened. "We're gonna go?"

"Of course," Joe blustered. "You don't think I'd let you down, do you?"

"No way!"

Darcy smiled but kept mum.

"Sometimes I wonder who's going to nag me into being a good father when you're gone," he said, keeping his eyes on the road. "It's going to be awfully quiet without you around."

"I'm sure you mean that in the nicest possible way," Darcy said as coolly as she could.

"I do." The two words hung in the air as they drove over mile after mile of twisting road.

When they got to the mall, they found it bustling with activity. The line to see Santa Claus was even longer than

Joe had feared it would be, and he found himself counting to ten for patience over and over again.

The line snaked around a maze of trellises covered with gold and silver garlands. The PA system piped thin strains of "Jingle Bells" and "Toyland" across the roar of parents and children chattering excitedly about presents or fussing over the lack of them.

Joe looked at Darcy over Ricky's head and said quietly, through his teeth, "Santa seems to be taking his time."

"That's how Santa works," she answered evenly.

Ricky tugged at Joe's shirt. "Can I go there and play?" He pointed to The North Pole Playground, a space about ten feet away where some children were playing around plastic reindeer.

"Okay," Joe said. "Just stay where you can see me." When Ricky had gone, he turned to Darcy and said sarcastically, "I'm *so* glad you suggested this."

She gaped at him, openmouthed. "Hey, it's not *my* fault the car broke down."

"I'm not so sure about that. When was the last time you had the oil changed?"

She cast him a withering stare. "For your information, I had new tires put on a couple of months ago. I'm sure the guys did it then."

"What guys?"

"The tire guys."

"Tire guys don't do oil."

"Why not?"

"They do *tires*. If you go for tires, you can't just expect to get oil. That makes no sense."

She shrugged impatiently. "They're all car guys."

"No, they're not. Tire guys do tires. Car guys are different."

Darcy rolled her eyes. "This is a stupid argument. So I didn't change the oil as often as you'd like. It's not like I put sugar in the gas tank or anything."

Joe gave a nod, but thought he wouldn't put it past Darcy to come up with a reason that seemed logical enough to warrant putting sugar in the tank.

"Besides," Darcy went on. "If it's anyone's fault, it's yours."

"Mine?"

"Obviously. If you'd been willing to nurture your child's dreams instead of ignoring them, I wouldn't have had to attempt that risky drive in the first place."

He stared at her, momentarily unable to form words. "Nurture his dreams?" he echoed. He swept his hand beside them, indicating the shiny plastic garlands, large white chunks of fake snow, and the meager display of plastic animals with which Ricky and the other children were playing. "You call this nurturing his dreams? If I had flat out refused to let him come here it would ultimately be better for him, not worse."

"You think so?"

A teenager dressed in an elf suit, smoking a cigarette, pushed past them and paused to crush the cigarette out on the floor.

"You think not?" Joe countered.

Darcy sadly looked at the elf, then in the direction of Ricky. She was glad to see Ricky wasn't looking back at them. Darcy turned her large eyes back to Joe. "I really thought this would be fun for him."

Joe paused, considering. "He's having a good time," he conceded.

Darcy drew a long breath, then spoke carefully. "All my life I wanted to go see Santa at the mall and my parents never let me. When you said no...well...I wanted Ricky to at least get the chance.''

The line edged forward and Joe looked across the expanse of people and shopping bags to the man sitting in the large golden throne, aptly labeled Santa's Seat. The old man had white hair and a real white beard that hung like steel wool down to his chest. His eyes were a startling pale blue and even from several yards away Joe could see they looked kind. Children came to sit on his lap and detail their wish lists, and as they spoke, their eyes lit up and their faces grew increasingly animated.

The mall was definitely not a place Joe would consider to be filled with Christmas spirit, but this small corner of it was. It would do Ricky some good to have his faith in something rewarded. Later he could learn the truth about Santa Claus. For now, underneath all the plastic decorations, shrill versions of Christmas carols, and cranky shoppers, this was a wonderful validation of the innocence of childhood.

And they had Darcy to thank for it.

''Dumb dwarf,'' she uttered, watching the teenager push through to the photo area. ''You'd think they'd have some sort of rules about smoking, wouldn't you?''

Joe smiled. ''Elf.''

She turned to him, uncomprehending. ''What?''

''He's an elf.'' The line inched forward. ''You said dwarf.''

She frowned and Joe noticed, for the first time, the fine curve of her brow. ''What's the difference?''

He gestured to the kid's feet. ''Elves wear pointy shoes.''

It was almost their turn, so Joe called Ricky back to join them in line.

"Is it my turn?" Ricky asked as he ran to them.

"Almost," Darcy told him.

"Do you know what you're going to say to Santa Claus?" Joe asked.

Ricky gave a secret smile and looked from his father to Darcy and back. "Yup."

"Aren't you telling?" Darcy asked.

"It's a secret." He looked unsure as to whether or not that was okay.

"Ahh." She gave Ricky a quick wink. "Just between you and the big man himself, huh?"

He nodded. "Is that okay?"

"It's fine," Joe reassured him. "There aren't many times it's a good idea to keep secrets from me, but this is one of the times that's okay."

Ricky brightened.

A young woman in a short red-and-green velvet dress and red velvet elf hat stepped forward. "Will you be wanting a picture taken?"

Joe looked at his son and didn't have to think. "Sure we will." As she loped away, he said to Ricky, "It's not every day you get a chance like this." The look in the boy's eye told him he was right, and that it mattered more than he ever would have dreamed possible.

When the elf indicated that it was Ricky's turn to go see Santa, he ran so quickly that he slipped on the spray-painted indoor/outdoor carpet, fell down, and got a red smudge on his jeans. Instead of fretting about it, though, he scrambled back to his feet and walked, a bit more carefully, the rest of the way.

Darcy and Joe stood back several feet, allowing Ricky the space to talk privately with Santa. Darcy had been

watching and had noticed that one of the parents usually
went to the old man afterwards and got the lowdown on
what the child wanted.

Ricky beamed for the camera, then whispered excitedly
in Santa's ear.

"What do you think he's saying?" Darcy asked Joe.

"Oh, the usual. Toy trucks, video games, anything re-
sembling a weapon."

It looked as if Santa asked Ricky a question, because
they both looked in the direction of Joe and Darcy then
and Ricky pointed right at her. Santa asked another question, and Ricky nodded enthusiastically.

"What do you suppose that was all about?" Darcy
asked.

Joe seemed to be wondering the same thing. "I have no
idea," he said slowly. "No idea."

Soon Ricky came bounding down the red carpet. They
were about to go to the photo counter, when Santa signaled
for Darcy to come to him.

"Me?" She pointed to herself.

The Santa nodded and summoned her again.

Joe and Ricky were deep in conversation about some
sort of robot transformer, so Darcy figured it would probably be best for her to find out what Ricky had asked for
and then tell Joe later.

"That's a nice young man," the Santa said to Darcy as
she approached. His eyes were even softer than they'd appeared from a distance.

"Yes, he is," Darcy agreed.

"Said there's only one thing he wants for Christmas this
year and that's a new mom."

Darcy felt her face grow warm. "His mother passed
away a couple of years ago."

Santa nodded, and she was touched by the compassion she saw in his expression. "He mentioned that."

"How can his father explain to him that Santa doesn't bring mothers for Christmas?" Darcy asked, picturing a workshop filled with Frankenstein elves building mothers from clay.

"The lad doesn't want just *any* mother." He was sounding more and more like Edmund Gwynn from *Miracle on 34th Street.* "He asked specifically for you."

"Me? He wants me to be his new mother?" Darcy laughed nervously.

"You are Darcy?"

She nodded.

"Then you'd be the one." He paused, surveying her with his sweet Christmas eyes, then added, "If this is an impossibility, then I suggest you and the boy's father make that clear to him as soon as possible. It seems he has his heart set on it."

"Yes, we'll do that." In truth, she had no idea how she could even begin to handle the situation. "Did he mention anything else he might want? Board games? Model airplane kits? Anything?"

The man shook his head, then pointed across the hall to a science and nature store. "But you'll find some dandy toys and educational games in there. Good stocking stuffers," he added, with what she could only describe as a merry twinkle, "if you'd like to give me some help this year."

For one disconcerting moment Darcy almost wondered if this man really might be Santa Claus. Then she heard Ricky call her from across the crowd and she turned to look. When she turned back to thank the Santa, he was already occupied with another child's hopes and dreams.

She made her way through the crowd. When she got to Joe and Ricky, she noticed they were holding big chocolate chip cookies they'd purchased from one of the mall vendors.

"We got you one," Ricky said, holding a warm cookie out to her.

"Mmm, thanks." She took a bite and met Joe's eyes. "Is this dinner?"

"Just an appetizer."

"Were you talking to Santa Claus, too?" Ricky asked. Darcy fumbled. "Yes, sort of."

"What did you tell him you want?"

As her eyes flicked to Joe, she stifled a momentary pang of longing. "Wisdom," she said.

"Is that all?" Joe asked her.

She took in his handsome, rugged appearance, realizing as she did that she was certainly in the company of the best-looking man at the mall. Something like pride bulged in her chest. "Strength, too," she answered. Before he could answer, or tempt her to say more, she looked down at Ricky. "What did you ask for?"

"It's a secret. I can't tell you and—" he turned to Joe "—I can't tell you. But I know Santa Claus will give it to me. It's the only time I've ever asked him for anything. *Anything.*"

Joe raised a questioning eyebrow to Darcy. She gave an answering nod and mouthed the word "Later."

He smiled in understanding and once again her heart did a useless flip. She reminded herself it was less than six weeks now before Joe and Ricky were leaving. If she could just hold out that long, they'd be gone and so would her unrealistic ideas about staying with them.

* * *

Fortunately, Ricky fell asleep in the car on the way home, so Joe and Darcy were able to talk quietly without disturbing him.

"So what did that guy say to you?" Joe asked as they drove through the town. He was feeling mighty skeptical about the whole "mall Santa" business again, especially since he'd seen the old man pointing to a pricey educational chain store.

"Oh, you won't believe what he said." She pinched the bridge of her nose with her thumb and forefinger.

"What?"

She glanced into the backseat, pressed her lips together, then said, "By the way, I was thinking—" she lowered her voice "—maybe I could do some of the Santa Claus shopping for Ricky so you wouldn't have to take time off from the ranch work. What do you think?"

"What did he say?" Joe persisted.

Her speaking got a little faster, a little higher pitched. "Because I've been spending a lot of time with him lately and I've got some great ideas for things he'd like. Okay?"

"Fine." Joe gave her a hard look. "Now tell me what the man said Ricky told him."

"All right, all right." She faced him, her expression clearly showing confusion even in the dim glow of the streetlights. "Ricky said he wants a new mother for Christmas."

Joe groaned. All of Ricky's words came back to him, along with the enthusiasm. "That's the thing he's sure Santa will bring since he's never asked for anything else?"

Darcy grimaced. "Well...not exactly. There's a little more to it."

He felt relieved. Somewhere he'd heard that the Lord

didn't close a door without opening a window. "Something I can do, I hope."

"Well...no. I mean, it's worse." She exhaled a pent-up breath.

"How much worse could it be?"

"Apparently Ricky wants *me* to be his new mother."

Joe was glad at that moment that they had left the illumination of the city lights and pulled onto the darkened country road, because he was certain the expression on his face must have been telling. "He said that? He specifically said that?"

"I'm afraid so."

Ricky had mentioned it to Joe, of course, but what Ricky said in private and what Ricky said in public were two different things. Usually. "So that's why he was pointing in our direction," he said flatly. "I should have known there was something strange about that."

Darcy sighed. "Oh, Joe, what are we going to do?"

"Short of getting married?"

She gave a humorless laugh. "Yeah."

"I mean, we learned a long time ago that we don't work. Didn't we?"

"Right." Her voice sounded flat. "So what do we say to Ricky?"

"I don't know." He thought about it. There were no consolation prizes when Ricky had his heart set on something. "I guess I'm just going to have to set him straight."

"Can I help somehow?"

Several answers came to mind. *You could marry me,* he might say. *I know it's a pretty quiet lifestyle but I think I could make you happy. Maybe.* But saying something like that to Darcy would be like committing emotional suicide, especially since she'd just said herself that they didn't "work" together. Joe had given her the perfect opening to disagree, but she hadn't taken it. And he wouldn't mention it again. He wasn't setting himself up for that sort of fall.

He shook his head. "Nah. I'm going to have to take care of this one myself."

Chapter Twelve

Ricky woke up in the car as soon as they got home. When they got inside, Joe noticed the light on the telephone answering machine was blinking. So while Ricky went to brush his teeth, wash his face and change into his pajamas, Joe checked for messages.

It was the real-estate agent. She had a prospective buyer who wanted to see the place first thing in the morning. She left a phone number and asked Joe to call her as soon as he got the message, no matter what the time.

He made a quick call to Darcy. "She needs to come by first thing in the morning. That okay by you?"

"First thing in the morning?" Darcy's voice sounded thin, tired. "I guess so. Gosh, that was fast."

"I know." Joe felt grim. "Lucky us, huh?"

"Yeah. Lucky."

When they hung up, Joe sat for a moment, wondering what it was that he'd heard in Darcy's voice. Was she just exhausted from the day, or was her reaction to showing the ranch less than enthusiastic? He dismissed that idea quickly. She'd made it clear that she was ready and willing to move on. For her, this was good fortune.

For him, too, he reminded himself.

Joe went to Ricky's room and sat down on the edge of the bed. He wasn't at all sure where to start, so he dove right in. "I noticed you were pretty excited about going out with Darcy tonight."

Ricky nodded, with a wholly unself-conscious smile. "I love her."

I love her. Joe was momentarily stunned by his son's declaration. How easy it was for Ricky to make such an admission. The boy had no idea how complicated that one statement became as years passed by.

With a deep breath, Joe composed himself and tried again. "Darcy has been a nice friend for us here, hasn't she?" Even to his own ears it sounded lame, but he couldn't come up with anything better.

"Yeah." Ricky ran his fingers along the tattered edge of his blanket, concentrating on that rather than on the conversation.

"But you and I aren't going to be staying here for much longer." Joe touched Ricky's cheek with a knuckle, drawing the boy's attention back. "You understand that, don't you?"

The boy nodded. "Unless you and Darcy get married," he said, and looked back at the blanket.

Joe's heart skipped a beat. Of course, this was exactly the kind of response he should have expected from Ricky, but it still threw him for a loop. He composed himself and used it to his advantage. "Interesting that you should bring that up," he said, as casually as he could manage. The vague thought crossed his mind that it was good Ricky had brought this up so that Santa Claus's myth would remain intact. "Because Darcy and I aren't going to get married."

"You're not?" Ricky's face was the picture of surprise. It was as though he'd been counting on it—*positive* of it. "Why not?"

"We never were, Rick. I'm not sure where you got that idea."

"You guys kissed." Ricky's voice gained force. "She said you needed to kiss more and then you could get married. So I thought you kissed more."

Joe ruffled his son's hair. "Is that *exactly* what she said?" he asked knowingly. "Were those the same words?"

After a moment's hesitation, Ricky's mouth quirked into a small, reluctant smile. They'd had this talk before, and he knew what his father was saying. "I don't know."

Joe laughed. "I don't think Darcy said to you, 'Your dad and I need to kiss more and then we'll get married.' Did she?"

"No," Ricky admitted.

Joe took his small hand. "But you wanted that to happen, so that's what you believed."

Ricky nodded shyly.

Joe expelled a long breath. "It's okay. All of us do that sometimes. We want something so badly that we figure if we just pretend it's true, it will be." He thought of the years he'd pretended he was happy in his marriage, and the fact that he'd never be able to be totally honest with Ricky about that. "But the truth is, wishing isn't enough to make something happen," he finished.

"What else do I have to do?" Clearly he was ready to do whatever it took.

"There's nothing else you can do about Darcy and me, or about anyone outside of yourself. Something like that just has to be right or else..." He looked for the words. "Or else it just isn't right."

Ricky nodded. "Then *you* have to make it happen."

"If I could make it right, I would," Joe said, looking out Ricky's bedroom window at the darkened main house in the distance. "Believe me, I would."

"I don't believe you."

Startled, Joe blurted, "What?"

"I don't think you're even trying." Tears threatened in the child's eyes.

For a moment, Joe was stunned into silence. "Like I told you, Ricky, something like this is between the two people involved. If it's right, they know it. If it's not, no amount of trying is going to change that."

"You just have to kiss more," he contended stubbornly. "Darcy told me."

Joe didn't want to tell Ricky that Darcy was wrong. But he also couldn't have him believing a family and security were so easily within his father's grasp. "That's just the beginning," he said. "That's only the beginning. After that, there's a lot more complicated stuff involved."

Ricky yawned and, moments later, fell asleep. Joe wasn't sure whether there was any further understanding. In a way he was glad, because he'd exhausted his very limited repertoire of relationship wisdom. But he was also disappointed. He wanted this conversation over, once and for all. He didn't want his son pining for a family he couldn't have.

Darcy couldn't be domesticated, he thought for what was at least the hundredth time. She was like a wild horse. She could be admired from afar but never be tamed.

His energy would be better spent on the problems of the ranch, he decided. Someone was coming to look at the place tomorrow. Meanwhile, there were horses to sell, fences to mend and a million other things to do before he left. Things that would take his mind off…desire.

And when those things were finally done, it would be time for him and Darcy to go their separate ways.

Darcy got out of bed with the first hint of dawn. There was no use trying to sleep anymore; she couldn't do it. She felt certain that the person—or people—who were coming to look at the ranch were going to buy it. And she felt rushed. She wasn't quite ready. That is, there were still so many things to do, to fix up.

She put on some warm clothes and crept through the big empty house. She didn't know why she crept, but the creaking floorboards somehow made her feel that she should.

Ghosts, she decided. The place was full of them. And she didn't want to disturb their slumber or, worse, wake them.

She went out to the barn. Already she'd been at the ranch longer than a month and she hadn't once gone riding. Something kept getting in the way of this great pleasure for her, but now was a good time. Riding had always helped her to sort her thoughts and soothe her.

Her footsteps echoed as she walked through the cavernous aisle of the main barn. There were soft whinnies and nickers from horses near and far. Soon the place would be teeming with hired hands, quickly and efficiently going through the motions of the morning feed, but now the silence was like a thick, warm blanket around her.

As she wandered through, she tried to remember what

she'd heard about the various horses—which ones were gentle, which were green. When she got to a stall marked with a placard that said "West," she paused. Hadn't there been a colt named West all those years ago? A beautiful bay with a blaze right down the center of his gentle face.

This horse was brown, but he was facing the window opposite Darcy.

"Hey, West." She clicked her tongue against her teeth but he didn't turn to face her. She reached in and rattled the feed bucket. That got his attention. He turned around and Darcy's heart sighed. It was him. An old horse, now. Eleven years old or so. A visual reminder of how much time had passed.

West had come from good stock, that much she recalled. "Let's go for a ride, okay, boy?" She put her hand out and he sniffed at it, then shook his head, rattling his halter. "I know, I know. How about a bribe?" She pulled a carrot from the back pocket of her jeans and fed it to him.

She led him out of the stall, listening to his iron shoes clopping loudly on the cement walkthrough. It was a sound she had always loved, but this morning it echoed, emphasizing the empty loneliness that was settling on the place.

Soon new faces would replace the old, and the True Love Ranch would become someplace different. It would become someone else's home, filled with someone else's memories. Eventually it would even harbor someone else's ghosts.

She clipped West at the cross ties and slipped into the tack room for his saddle and bridle. The overhead bulb produced a warm but dim glow, and for a moment Darcy could almost picture Joe in the corner, smiling devilishly at her as if to say, "What took you so long?"

Another ghost, another memory. It would do her good

to get away from here after the sale. San Diego would chase away all those memories; she'd have a life there, and wouldn't need old fantasies. She went back to West, whose ears pricked at the sound of the jingling bridle.

"We won't be long," she said, slipping the reins over his head. She slid the snaffle bit between his teeth, reflecting that he wouldn't have such a mild bit if he were a wild horse—though he did look as if he had a good amount of life in him. She wasn't about to wake Joe and ask him about West. "We'll just go out for a little bit, then you can have your breakfast, boy."

She untwisted the reins, tossed them over the horse's head, then secured the throat latch. For a moment, she considered the saddle that she had just carried out, then decided against it and led him outside to an overturned feed bucket. "Now, you hold still." She stepped on the bucket and jumped onto the horse's back.

Immediately, he sprang to life, sidestepping and bouncing until Darcy loosened the rein and bent down toward his ear. "Easy now." When she squeezed her legs to put pressure on his flanks, he stopped. He walked calmly through the paddock, responding to Darcy's every signal.

When they got into the main field, she bent forward and patted West's neck. His ears flicked backwards to listen to her. "Go for it," she whispered, and nudged him gently with her heel. It was all the persuasion he needed. With a couple of warm-up strides, he was running at a full gallop across the rolling fields, toward the misty hilltop.

Darcy's long-dormant instincts came back to life. Like someone riding a bike after many years, she had no trouble maintaining her balance or control. She rested her hands on the rough mane at West's neck and breathed deeply the scents of musky horse and cold air. It was like a drug; everything suddenly felt right for the first time in days.

She tried to clear her mind and ride like the wind, leaving all her troubles behind her. But thoughts of Joe clung to her like a tangled vine. She tried to shake free of them. Joe and Ricky would be at the ranch when she got back, she could think about them then. Hopefully she would even bring some perspective with her.

The last tiny bright stars were still winking in the sky when they got to the hilltop. West was breathing heavily, great puffs of white bursting from his nose. Darcy squeezed her thighs against the warm body and bent down to pat the horse's withers again. "Good boy," she said. She looked across the familiar land and thought of the prospective buyers coming to look at it today. Of course they'd buy—how could anyone resist it? Tears burned in her eyes and she bent down over the horse's neck. "I wonder if you'll miss it here, too."

His ears flicked back toward her voice, but she had lost the words. All around her, the landscape spread like a familiar painting. Though it had been years since she'd been here, it still represented safety, security. She sniffed and rubbed the dampness from her eyes. Even while the land beckoned, a voice inside her said, "It's time to let go."

"I don't want to let go," she said to West. "I could have had a chance to make the ranch work, but I failed." She sighed and shook her head. The wind picked up and blew like cold fingers through her hair.

She thought, for the hundredth time that day, of Ricky. She pictured the little cherub face, and the huge trusting eyes. She pictured the child walking heavily to bed at night, holding her hand for support and murmuring "I love you" in a small, sleepy voice as she tucked him in. It hadn't happened, but she really wanted it to. She wanted to keep Ricky in her life. She pictured the sleeping child as she had seen him before Thanksgiving by the half light of the night-light, protectively clutching his worn and tattered stuffed animal.

Maybe she *could* make them happy, she thought, but she'd never know. There was no room in a child's life or heart for that sort of guessing game. Joe had to maintain for Ricky whatever security he could, and that didn't include any sort of 'trial period' with a very dubious mother figure. She would only make a mess of it all the way she had everything else in her life.

Darcy straightened her back and turned West toward home. This time the horse walked at an easy, comfortable pace. She kept her eyes on the yellow glow in the windows of Joe's tenant house. It looked so cozy.

She made several detours along the way back, telling herself she needed to check out the condition of the property, but knowing in her heart that she was afraid to go back and face Joe. Nothing had changed as far as *he* knew, but she was afraid he would read her longing in her face.

By the time she got back to the barn the sun was high in the sky, and Darcy had convinced herself, once again, that selling the ranch was for the best.

When she walked the horse into the barn, she was surprised to see Joe there, covered in muck and what looked like blood.

"My God, what happened?" Darcy gasped.

"Ladybug finally decided to have her foal at the crack of dawn this morning." He wiped a dirty forearm across his brow. "Where the heck have you been?"

"I went for a ride." She looked at her watch and started:

she'd been gone for hours. "I guess I was gone longer than I realized."

"Long enough for a new life to come into the world." He gestured toward the stall, and Darcy walked over to see the small, feeble creature trying to nurse at Ladybug. "We have a new stallion from excellent stock, or at least we will in a couple of years. I mean, someone will."

Darcy watched the foal in wonder. "Wow" was all she could manage at first. "It's not going to be easy to let them go, is it?"

"It's not going to be easy to let any of this go," Joe said, walking to the water pump. He turned the pump on and rinsed his arms, hands, and face. When he finished he turned back to Darcy. "Not easy at all."

"It's not as though you have any choice. Is it?" Darcy asked, without looking at him. She concentrated, instead, on the wobbly foal before her.

"I guess not." He studied her for a moment, then amended that. "Obviously not. I can't buy you out and you can't buy me out."

"Even if we wanted to," she said, with a lift to her voice that let him know it was a question.

Apparently he didn't pick up on it, because he nodded. "It's too bad."

She tried to agree but the words wouldn't come out.

Joe looked at the mare and foal. "Don MacMahon down at the Double X has had his eye on this mare for some time now. Asked me to call when she foaled." He glanced at Darcy. "It's a pretty sure sale if you don't have any objections."

She looked at the mare and the nursing foal. It seemed as if everyone and everything was more capable of having family ties than she was. "No," she said in a strong voice. "No, not at all. That's good news."

Joe gave a quick nod and patted the mare's withers. "Guess I'll go make that call then." He hesitated outside the stall door and looked at Darcy. "The sooner we start selling the livestock off, the better, right?"

"Right." She didn't meet his eyes. "Absolutely."

Instead of going in to the phone, he shifted his weight from one foot to the other. "You're already outta here mentally, aren't you?"

She nodded without enthusiasm. "We're all just about gone."

Joe went in to the long-familiar tack room, sat down heavily on the chair by the phone and made the call. Dan MacMahon was thrilled with the prospect of taking on the mare and young foal, and he offered a price even higher than Joe had dared hope for. Joe tried to feel elated, but he couldn't muster much heart for the sale.

With a weary sigh, he hung up the receiver and looked around the room.

He'd spent many romantic nights in this very room with Darcy all those years ago. He could still picture her carefully drawing the shades so the light wouldn't show to anyone outside.

Those had been some wonderful days. First love. He would never forget the feeling of waiting for her on a sultry summer night, and the thrill of seeing her coming toward him through the darkness. Yes, she'd been his first love...his only love if he told himself the truth.

But that had been a long time ago, before he realized how crucial differences like theirs were. Before he realized how important it was for two people to come from similar backgrounds and to want similar things from life.

This place is the past for me and it's going to stay that way. Her words came back to him. It *was* the past; he would have to get it through his own head.

"Joe?" he heard Darcy call from the other side of the door. "The foal's standing by himself, you have to see this. Joe? Come here, quick."

He stood and went to the tack room door. It had slammed shut behind him when he'd come in and now it was stuck. Some things never changed. He counted silently to three, then hurled his weight against the door.

The door swung open and smacked firmly into something. *Darcy!* Before Joe had even a moment to act, she fell to the ground, unconscious.

Chapter Thirteen

Darcy's head felt as if it had split wide open. Pain throbbed through her brain in wave after wave. She was lying on something icy cold and hard. Familiar wooden beams crisscrossed overhead. The barn? Yes, she'd been in the barn. She closed her eyes. She needed sleep.

"Darcy?" She was vaguely aware of someone saying her name, but it sounded so far away. "Darcy? Darcy, talk to me. Darcy, squeeze my hand if you can hear me."

Was someone's hand in hers? She concentrated. Yes, she could feel a warm hand gripping hers. With effort she squeezed.

There was an audible sigh of relief from the other person. Slowly, she opened her eyes. Joe's face came into focus as though it were the light at the end of a long tunnel. "What—?" She swallowed and tried again. Nausea bubbled in her throat. "What happened?"

"I opened the tack room door and hit you in the head," he answered. Then there was just a trace of a smile. "Or you hit the door. I'm not exactly sure which. You called out to me."

She closed her eyes, remembering. "The foal," she murmured. Speaking was an incredible effort.

"Darcy?" His voice was suddenly stiff with concern.

She winced in pain.

"Okay, don't say too much." He put her arm gently on the ground and moved his hand down her body. "Can you feel this?" he asked, tapping her upper thigh.

"Is this a...pass?" She showed her teeth; it was as close to a smile as she could get. How embarrassing to be lying out cold on the floor of the barn. With Joe, of all people.

"It's whatever you want it to be, sweetheart. Just tell me you're okay." He moved down to her shins and feet, asking, "This? How about this?"

When he had tested all of her extremities and was apparently satisfied that she hadn't suffered any spinal damage, he said, "Do you think you can get up?"

She was already moving that way, although slowly. "I'm fine, really." She raised a hand to her head and closed her eyes for a moment. "But what a whack in the head that was!"

He slid his hand under her neck and down to her shoulder blade. "I'm so sorry."

"What happened?" It was one of the hired hands, his voice sharp with worry. "What's wrong with her?"

"I clobbered her in the head with the tack room door," Joe replied, then added, unnecessarily, "Accidentally."

"Is she all right?" another voice asked. Darcy was vaguely aware of the sounds of many footsteps rushing toward them.

"Seems to be, although she's going to have some goose

egg there. I'm going to take her out to the hospital so they can give her the once-over.''

Ricky.

She must have said the word aloud because Joe said, ''He's at school already, don't worry about it.''

Darcy relaxed a little. ''Good. What about the real-estate agent?''

''Shhh.'' Joe shifted his hold on her and began walking. She was vaguely aware of being hoisted into the cold leather passenger seat of Joe's Blazer and then being strapped in. ''The agent can do the job herself. We're just going to make sure you're okay now.''

The trip to the hospital passed in a blur for Darcy. All she could remember later was that every time she started to slip into the blissful sleep that kept pulling her in, Joe would reach over and slap her shoulder or pinch her and say, ''Wake up. Stay awake. Look out the window and try and keep track of all the red cars you see.''

She wanted to laugh. He was treating her like a child, but she thought she understood why. ''You think it's a concussion?'' she asked, raising her hand to shield her eyes from the bright sunlight.

''Yep. Now stay awake.''

''Bossy,'' she said, then started trying to count red cars.

It turned out that she did have a concussion, and a tremendous, ugly lump on her head. Worse, the only way she could go to sleep was if someone stayed around to wake her every two hours. Joe volunteered for the job and assured the doctor that he would take good care of her.

By the time they left the hospital it was after noon.

''Sorry to put you to all this trouble,'' Darcy said, feeling considerably better than she had on the way in. She must have gotten a second wind, she thought.

"I didn't want to work today anyhow," Joe said, then yawned. "You gave me the perfect excuse. Just don't tell my partner."

She leaned her head against the headrest and looked out the window. The sun was high in the sky now, and there were no clouds. She recalled the sight of the newborn foal nursing at its mother. "Amazing."

"What's that?"

She turned toward Joe. His dark hair was ruffled as though he'd run his hand through it repeatedly while he waited for her. His face was a shade paler than usual, but he didn't have the hideous dark circles that she knew she had. In fact, he looked pretty sensational. It figured. "New life," she said in answer to his question. "I'd never get tired of witnessing something like that. I wish I'd been there during the birth."

"You and me both," he agreed.

Only then did she realize that he was still in his grungy clothes. "You must be dying for a shower," she said.

"*You* must be dying for me to *take* one."

She smiled but shook her head. "Nah, you're okay." A few miles passed in silence. "Do you think this was some sort of sign?"

He drew to a halt at a red light and turned to look at her very seriously. "Meaning what?"

Meaning I should stay here, she thought, and that I belong here along with you and Ricky. But she couldn't say it. "Oh, I don't know," she replied. "Just talking nonsense."

He didn't respond. The light changed and he drove on,

through town and onto the one-lane country road that led to True Love Ranch.

When he reached the house, he stopped the car and turned the ignition off.

"You don't have to walk me up," Darcy said. "You must be anxious to get back to your place and grab some sleep. I know I am," she added, under her breath.

"That's right," he said. "That's exactly why I'm staying. I said I would stick around and wake you up every two hours and that's what I'm going to do."

She waved the notion away with her hand, but she wondered just how dangerous it would be to fall asleep. "I'll be fine," she said without conviction.

"Did you hear that?"

"What?"

"I heard it."

"Heard what?"

"That little dip in your voice just now when you said you'd be fine. The one that means you don't mean a word you're saying. I remember that."

"Don't be absurd."

"I've heard it before," Joe said with a shake of his head. He got out, walked around to her side, and opened the door. "Come on. We have a long day ahead."

"Are you going to try to keep me awake? Because I have to warn you, I'm not warm to that idea at all."

"You can sleep." He clamped a firm hand on her shoulder and urged her out of her seat. "Just in very small increments. Don't worry, I'll take care of you."

"Joe, I'm a grown woman. You don't need to take care of me." She tripped over one of the stones on the pathway and Joe grabbed her. The feel of his strong arms around her made her tingle with pleasure. Evidently not all of her was exhausted. In her current state, he might be more than she could resist.

"Darcy, I'm responsible for you being in this condition. So I'm responsible for seeing you through." They stopped at the front door.

"I could use some coffee," Darcy said with a skeptical frown. "Do you think you could possibly make a drinkable cup of brew?"

"Of course."

"Okay then." She smiled and opened the door. "You can stay."

Ten minutes later, Darcy was upstairs changing her clothes, and Joe was in the kitchen, trying to figure out how much coffee he should put in the machine. The fancy gourmet coffee bag had no instructions on it whatsoever. He opened it up and sniffed. It didn't smell very strong. He filled the filter about halfway, then fitted the filter back into the machine and looked for the place to pour the water. He was sure he'd seen people do it that way, and there was obviously a hollow section that could hold the water, but there was no clear way to get it in. He stood there for several minutes holding the pot of clear water and studying the machine.

There was no way he was going to ask Darcy.

Finally he decided to just boil the water and dip the coffee-filled filter in. That was the way it worked with tea. By the time Darcy got downstairs, he had put the glass pot of dark liquid back on the hot plate of the machine.

"Coffee ready?" she asked wearily.

"Ready and waiting," he answered with a quick glance from the machine to her. "Have a seat and I'll pour you some."

She sat down at the table and noticed the card that the real-estate agent had left. Darcy picked it up and examined it for a long time before dropping it back on the table and putting her head down. When she spoke, her voice was muffled.

"What?" he asked, pouring slightly lumpy black liquid into a mug.

She lifted her head. "I said, they've been here. We'll probably be hearing from the agent this afternoon."

He looked around the kitchen and expelled a heavy sigh. "Yup, you're probably right. We sure got this place whipped into shape. It's a steal."

"Do you think we should raise the price?"

He shrugged. "Marjorie thinks it's already high, as the market goes."

"Well, it doesn't seem like enough to me."

"I know," he said quietly. "Me, neither."

A long silence passed between them.

After a few minutes, Darcy said, "It's going to be Christmas in a few weeks. Time has gone by so fast."

He took out a spoon and stirred the coffee, hoping the lumps would dissolve. "I know. But I still feel like there's so much to do."

She nodded. "I think it's always like that. You could work on a house forever, just like an oil painting. The work is never finished, just abandoned for something else."

"Like California."

"Or Oklahoma," she countered.

He splayed his arms in surrender. "So how about your coffee? What do you want in it?" he asked, looking dubiously in the cup.

She ran her hands over her eyes. "Just black today, thanks."

He set the cup down on the table in front of her and said, "Are you anxious to get out to California?"

As if in response, wind blew against the window panes; they both knew it was a cold one.

Darcy started to lift the coffee mug, then set it down. "I don't know."

"You don't know?"

She shrugged. "I don't know anything right now. I'm so exhausted I can barely remember my name. Maybe I should skip the coffee and go straight to bed."

"Let me help you up, then."

She waved him off. "I just got back down. Coffee'll perk me up some."

"Undoubtedly." He watched her hand hovering near the handle of her mug. "But maybe you'd prefer tea?"

She pinched the bridge of her nose and stifled a yawn. "No, this is fine. You know what worries me?"

"What?"

"What if the people who want to buy the ranch want to tear down the house? You hear about that all the time. Do you think we can put a stipulation in the contract?"

He looked doubtful. "I don't know about that."

"Still...maybe one of us should stay on here and see the sale through. Just to make sure it goes to people who will love it. Maybe I'll stay."

He leaned forward. "Would you really consider that?"

"Why not?"

"Wouldn't you be bored, staying on in this one-horse town indefinitely?"

She eyed him evenly. "I haven't been bored so far."

Joe remained calm, but his mind raced with questions. Was it possible that he'd been wrong about Darcy's need to be on the move?

"Could you spend the rest of your life here?" He didn't realize he'd asked the question out loud until he saw her head jerk up, eyes wide.

"The rest of my life?" She swallowed. "What are you asking?"

He studied the rim of his coffee mug. "Nothing, nothing. What I meant was, could you commit to staying here indefinitely while this place is on the market?"

"Commit to it?" she repeated quietly. "Is that a commitment?"

"I suppose it could be." He shrugged. "You know, if you stayed on, we wouldn't have to hire a foreman to keep an eye on the hired hands and what not. If you agreed to stay and then, say, decided to leave suddenly, we might find ourselves in trouble." He watched her lift the coffee cup again.

She set the cup down and rolled her eyes. "Is that the sort of person you think I am? A..." What was the expression? she thought. "A fly-by-night?"

He laughed and shook his head. He was inches away from explaining to her *exactly* what he was asking her, but he wasn't sure what he'd say to her after that. What if she said she could stay on forever? What if she said she loved the idea of having a family and home? Could he say to her that he'd stay, too?

He didn't know the answer. He had a little bit of money left over now and could begin to pay Rosanna what he owed her if he stayed on to work the ranch, but what if it didn't earn money? How would he pay Rosanna back then?

It was a hell of a chance to take.

"What are you getting at?" she asked him.

"I'm not getting at anything," he said after a thoughtful pause. "Just making conversation."

"Oh."

Was it his imagination or did he read disappointment in her face? "So how's your head?"

"Better." She raised the mug of coffee again and finally took a sip. The face she made in reaction was more eloquent than any words could have been. "What *is* this?"

"It's coffee."

"No, it's not."

"It's not?"

Darcy dipped her finger in, swirled it for a moment, then pulled it out and studied the small brown flakes. "But it seems to have coffee *in* it." She set the cup down and pushed it away. "What in the world did you do to it? It's even worse than the stuff you made at your place."

Joe paused. "I'm not much of a coffee drinker."

She raised an eyebrow, then nodded. "I don't doubt it." She pushed her chair back from the table and carried the cup to the sink. "Is your tea any better?"

"Marginally."

"You need a wife," she said with a laugh, ther immediately looked stricken. "Not that a wife would.. " Sh fumbled for words, then finally pointed to her head. "Did I mention I have a head injury?"

"I think I heard that somewhere."

She rinsed the mucky cup out and took a new filter out of the cabinet. "You should at least get a cook so that child of yours doesn't starve." She took the bag of coffee from the refrigerator, frowned and shook it. The bemused look she shot at Joe spoke volumes. "This was almost full this morning."

He nodded. "It was almost full half an hour ago."

She smiled and scooped three spoonfuls into the filter. "You're hopeless in the kitchen."

He eyed her. "Ah, but I'm masterful in other rooms."

"So you say."

"Try me."

"Very funny."

He watched with interest while she lifted the entire top of the coffee machine off and poured water in. So that was how it was done, he thought.

She turned to him. "Would you like some lunch?"

"Sure. I'll make it."

"No, no, no. I'm not about to let you try your hand at food after what you did to the coffee."

She refused to sit down even though he implored her, so he watched as she moved around the kitchen effortlessly making coffee and hot, cheesy omelets. He'd never dreamed she was capable of such domesticity.

He tried to remember what else had happened that day—something that had surprised him in a similar way... It hit him. She had asked about Ricky. She was knocked unconscious and taken, delirious, to the hospital. Yet she had thought to ask about Ricky before they left.

He watched her with something like awe as she moved about the kitchen, admiring her deft hands and smooth, graceful capability. He wasn't quite as hopeless in the kitchen himself as his coffee suggested, but at the same time he had never been able to get everything on the table hot. It might not take a "female touch," but it certainly took a talent that he didn't possess.

"I really wish you'd get some sleep, Darcy," Joe said after she'd bustled around for about fifteen minutes, cooking and then putting things away. "I feel like a complete dog sitting here while you work like this despite your injury. At least let me do the cleaning up.''

''No, I—''

He stood and took the pan out of her hands. ''You need to sleep,'' he said firmly. ''Now come on, I won't take 'no' for an answer.''

That seemed to be all the persuasion she needed, because she let him guide her upstairs to her room. She lay down on top of the bed and watched him as he went to the windows and lowered the shades. ''So you're going to stick around and make sure I don't die while I'm asleep?'' She was making a joke, but there was a thin line of childlike fear in her voice.

''I'll be right downstairs,'' he assured her.

''You'll be bored.'' She yawned broadly.

He gave a quick shake of his head. ''I'll use the phone to make some calls.''

''Including the realtor,'' she said sleepily. ''Don't forget that.''

She was drifting off to sleep quickly, he observed in relief. He took a crocheted afghan off the rocking chair by the window and laid it across her carefully. ''I won't forget the realtor,'' he assured her. Her eyes were closed. ''Darcy?''

Her only answer was a deep, rhythmic breathing.

He studied her sleeping form for a few minutes, then said, quietly, ''Good night, sweetheart,'' and bent to kiss her cheek. He would come back and check on her every forty-five minutes or so. If he stayed in here and watched her sleep for long, heaven only knew what foolish things he would admit to her when she woke up.

He was almost out the door when he stopped and looked back. To his own surprise, he heard himself say, ''I love you, Darcy Beckett.''

Chapter Fourteen

Two days before Christmas, Joe got another call from the realtor. There was a buyer, she told him delightedly. A businessman from Hawaii, who would be in town for only a couple of days over Christmas. He didn't even need to see the place—the pictures and dimensions were sufficient. He wanted to settle quickly and would pay them their full asking price, including for livestock, if they could close the deal on the day after Christmas.

"We couldn't have asked for better luck," Darcy said lamely when she heard the news.

They were giving the stabled horses their morning feed. Outside, the hired hands piled hay into the fields for the heartier horses outside.

"No," Joe agreed without enthusiasm. "It's lucky all right."

"Looks like you'll be able to leave on schedule." She pressed her lips together.

For just a moment, Joe thought he saw a glimmer in her eyes, but she blinked it away.

"You'll be in Oklahoma before the new school term," she added.

"Seems like it." He cleared his throat. "I'm not looking forward to telling Ricky, though."

"Doesn't he want to go?" Her voice was full of compassion.

Joe shook his head. "It's always hard to move, especially for a kid who's so young and has spent his whole life thinking of this as home."

Darcy nodded but didn't say anything. They worked side by side for a few minutes, carrying feed to the buckets down the long line of stalls.

"He'll miss you," Joe said without meeting Darcy's eyes. "A lot."

"I'll miss him, too."

He heard her give a quick sniff, but when he turned to face her she was looking away, concentrating on pouring feed into a bucket.

"The horses will probably miss you, too," Joe hedged.

"I'm not sure *that's* true."

"You and West have become great friends over the last few weeks."

"Yes, I suppose we have." She sniffed again. "So what time are you guys coming up for Christmas dinner?"

"Whenever you want. Say, four?"

"Perfect."

"Are you sure I can't bring anything?"

She laughed. "Quite sure. But thanks."

The small talk was killing him but he couldn't bring himself to say what was on his mind. "So I'll tell the agent we agree to the sale terms."

"That's probably best."

"Probably?"

"No. I mean yes. It's best." She dropped the bucket she was holding and looked at Joe with tears in her eyes. "It's all we can do...isn't it?"

He put his own bucket down and went to her slowly. "Do you want to stay?"

"It's not possible."

"That's not an answer."

"It's the only one I can give you. What's the point in pining for something that can't ever happen?"

"Like keeping the ranch?"

"For one thing, yes."

He stepped closer still and reached out to touch her chin. "Is there another thing? Is there something else you want?"

"There's a lot I want."

To his utter amazement, Darcy reached out, grabbed him by the shoulders and drew him into her. She kissed him, lightly at first, then fiercely, tightening her arms around him hard. Not that he had any objections. He rested his hands on her hip bones and pulled her closer.

Their mouths locked together in silent communication.

They were still for one suspended moment, then Darcy drew back.

Joe tried to collect his thoughts. "Darcy, do you want to call off the sale of the ranch? We can do that, you know." He wondered if that was, in fact, true. "Maybe we could work it out."

"How?" she implored. "The bank would foreclose within months if we stayed here. I've sunk every penny I have into it, and I think you've done pretty much the same."

He couldn't argue with that, he realized. "But maybe we could get a loan to get us on our feet."

"That would amount to the same thing. We talked about this in the beginning, remember? The ranch is already heavily mortgaged. If we took out a second mortgage and couldn't make it work quickly, the bank would foreclose and we'd be even more broke than we are now."

She was right. It was impossible. And pointless, considering that they both already had good, viable plans for moving on. But what about the possibility of Darcy going with him to Oklahoma? He pushed the idea away. It was unthinkable Darcy having to go to a ranch that was truly in the middle of nowhere and to stay with him while he paid off his debt to his former sister-in-law. He would manage, and it would be okay for Ricky because Rosanna was family and he was too young to feel the pinch. But Joe couldn't bear the idea of putting Darcy through such an ordeal.

So what about going with her to California? The thought of *that* almost made him laugh. He couldn't possibly impose himself on her that way. What was Darcy going to do with a rancher and a child out in La-La Land?

"You're right," he said sadly. "But it would have been nice."

Joe knew how important this Christmas was to Darcy after she'd worked so hard to make it special for Ricky. They'd been so busy with last-minute details for the sale that she and Ricky had only done little in the way of decorating—a sprig of holly here and there and a wreath hung on the door.

Joe had bought a tree a couple of days ago, and had tried fruitlessly to come up with an excuse to get her out of the house. He wanted to bring it in as a surprise. Finally, he decided to get Ricky in on it. He would ask Darcy to

take Ricky to see a special Christmas display in a nearby
town. Three hundred and sixty-four days a year the town
was called Ivy, but on Christmas it dubbed itself Christmas
Village, and people would drive from miles around to see
it.

"But I have to cook dinner," Darcy objected.

"What's to do? You stick the turkey in the oven and
wait five or six hours."

She smiled. "No offense, Joe, but you're hardly one to
be dispensing cooking tips."

"Am I wrong?"

"Yes."

"No, I'm not."

"What about all the side dishes?"

"You do that an hour before dinner," he said, trying to
usher her out the door. "I saw you do it at Thanksgiving.
Ricky, put on your coat."

She narrowed her eyes. "Are you trying to get rid of
me for some reason?"

"Yes, now will you go?"

She looked at Ricky. "Do you really want to see this
Christmas Village or are you part of your dad's plan to
get me out of the house?"

For once Ricky didn't spill the beans. "I want to see
Christmas Village," he said, all innocence.

Darcy relented, but this time she took Joe's car. He
couldn't afford to take the time to pick them up; there was
far too much to do and too little time as it was.

By the time they got back, three and a half hours later,
Joe was exhausted from his efforts, but the house looked
just like a picture from a magazine.

Ricky came in the door alone.

"Where's Darcy?" Joe asked, looking outside at the

sky, which had turned steel gray while they were gone. The air smelled metallic, he thought. Like snow.

"She's getting presents from the car." Ricky stepped inside and pulled his coat off. "She's got a huge one for you."

"She does?" He felt an odd twisting in his heart. "Where did you find a store that was open?"

"In Christmas Village."

That figured. If any place would have an open store on Christmas Day, it would be a place called Christmas Village.

"Talking about me?" At that moment, Darcy showed up in the doorway, fresh faced, with pink cheeks and bright eyes. Her hair tumbled in big curls around her shoulders and she was, indeed, holding an enormous box. "We had a great time, didn't we, Ricky?"

"Uh-huh." Ricky turned back to Joe. "You should have come."

Darcy handed the bulky package to Joe. "Merry Christmas," she said. "Looks like snow," she added hopefully. "When was the last time you had a white Christmas here?"

Ricky said, "We've never had a white Christmas." He thought for a moment. "What's a white Christmas?"

"That means a snowy Christmas." Darcy stopped and listened to the silence. "We need a little Bing around here. Do you have some music?"

Music! Damn, how could he have forgotten? He didn't have so much as a single tape. "I don't have any." He shrugged. "Maybe the radio..."

Darcy shook her head good-naturedly. "Don't worry, I've got some upstairs. I'll be back in a jiffy." She ran up the stairs and reappeared a moment later with a shoebox overflowing with tapes. "This ought to last a while."

He took the box from her and led them into the decorated drawing room. "I thought you didn't like Christmas."

"What I said was that I'd never had a particularly good one," Darcy corrected. "But hope springs eternal." Her eyes widened as she beheld the huge evergreen decorated with colored lights. "Joe," she breathed. "It's incredible."

Ricky ran immediately to a tiny train set that was circling the base of the tree, through small barns and houses that looked like something out of Dickens.

"How did you have time to do all of this?" She looked around her at the garlands hanging along the crown moldings, and the lights strung delicately through them. She walked slowly toward the fireplace and fingered the small wax figures of Santa and tiny elves on the mantel.

Joe suddenly felt embarrassed. "I didn't do it all today. It was ready, over at my place."

"You did all this for *me?*" She looked incredulous.

He shrugged, feeling his face grow hot. "I thought it would be nice to have the place decorated in case any potential buyers came through, but then when it sold...I figured I might as well surprise you with it."

"Well, you did," she said. "The tree..." Her eyes widened as she wandered around the huge icon, stopping every once in a while to take it all in.

"I didn't have any ornaments," Joe tried to explain. "But I thought it looked pretty nice with the lights on it."

"It's beautiful."

Joe popped a tape into the tape player and pushed a

button. "I'm glad you like it." The sound of Nat King Cole singing "The Christmas Song" floated into the air.

Darcy walked over to one of the old chintz chairs and draped herself across it. "This is great. And smell that turkey." She inhaled deeply. "Did you baste it the way I told you?"

"No problem."

She stood up and stretched luxuriously. "Then I'd better get everything else together. You guys hungry?"

"I had Cap'n Crunch for breakfast," Ricky chirped from his place by the train set. "But I'm still hungry."

"I'm not surprised," Darcy said. "Come on in and get a hunk of cheese or some sort of protein to keep you going while I fix dinner." She flashed Joe a look, but couldn't help smiling.

Ricky followed her into the kitchen and she gave him some cheese and crackers and a glass of milk. He brought them out and ate in front of the tree, while Joe relaxed on the couch.

Before he knew it, Joe had fallen asleep.

When he woke up, Darcy was shaking him. "Joe, where's Ricky?" she was asking.

He sat bolt upright. "He was..." He looked at the empty plate and glass in front of the tree, then glanced to the window. It was dark out. "What time is it?"

Darcy told him and his heart began to pound. He got up and went through the house with long strides, calling Ricky.

"He's probably playing hide-and-seek," Joe said to Darcy, then called Ricky's name again in a very loud voice.

"I'll look around here," Darcy said. Her voice shook with fear. "You go look at your place." He followed her gaze to the window, and they both looked at the dark ten-ant house. "Maybe he's down there."

Half an hour later, Joe and Darcy had turned both houses upside down to no avail.

"Joe, I'm scared," Darcy said. "We should call the police, get some sort of search party together."

He was about to agree when he remembered the barns. "Wait." He snapped his fingers. "I have an idea of where he might be." He ran out of the house without bothering to put a coat on.

Darcy followed.

It had begun to snow and already there was a light dust-ing of white on the landscape. Joe's heart pounded in his throat. If this hunch was wrong, he didn't know what he was going to do. He couldn't even entertain the thought. Ricky would be there. He *had* to be there.

"Ricky?" He slammed the barn door open and heard the horses spring to life. "Ricky?"

He thought he heard something. He stopped and stood very still. He heard Darcy's hard breathing behind him. "Ricky?" he called again.

"Dad?" a tiny voice came in response.

The feed room. Darcy and Joe ran to the feed room, and Joe switched on the light.

Ricky sat huddled in the corner, clutching his time-worn teddy bear close to him. He was wearing a coat, thank goodness, and his wool hat, askew, on his head.

Darcy got to him before Joe did, and gathered him in her arms. "Oh, Ricky, Ricky, we were so worried. What on earth are you doing out here?"

"N-not going back in."

"You're not going back in?" Joe repeated. "What are you talking about? Why not?"

"D-don't want to m-move to Clokahoma."

Neither of them corrected him.

"Why not?" Darcy asked gently. Joe was glad because he could barely find words to respond. "Why don't you want to go see your aunt in Oklahoma? It sounds like such fun."

"I wanna stay *here*," Ricky cried. "I want to stay with *you*."

Darcy looked as if she'd been caught off guard by the intensity of Ricky's words, Joe thought.

"Maybe you could write me letters and send me pictures when you get there," she suggested. "How about that?"

Ricky shook his head fervently. "I want to stay home."

"We're going to have a new home," Joe tried.

"No! *This* is home. I don't wanna go!" He dissolved into pathetic sobs then, and Joe went and lifted the child from Darcy's arms. He almost felt like crying himself, watching this sweet little soul in so much torment.

Ricky cried against his father's shoulder as they walked back to the house. Darcy was right next to them, and kept reaching up to pat the boy's shoulder or head.

"It will be okay," Joe heard her saying, over and over again, but she didn't sound as if she believed it.

Joe sighed. He had to find a way to make it all okay, not just for Ricky but for himself as well. And for Darcy, who had been looking especially unhappy ever since they found out they had a buyer for the ranch.

Joe knew he had to make it okay for everyone.

Chapter Fifteen

The house was warm and cozy when they got back inside. They were all famished, but Darcy had left in such haste that she'd forgotten the food. The turkey was dry and the side dishes she'd been warming in the oven were burned. Joe said not to worry, that he had an idea. Darcy sat Ricky by the fire and made him a cup of hot cocoa while Joe ran over to his place to get dry clothes for his son.

When he came back he produced two frozen pizzas. "Christmas dinner à la Tyler," he said with a smile, but his face was pale and drawn.

Darcy saw that she, too, needed to try and keep the mood light; otherwise Christmas was going to be a complete bust for all of them. "It's not Julia Child but it will surely do."

"You haven't seen the best of it." Joe held up a fancy tin of instant coffee. "I'm making the coffee tonight." He tapped the label. "Directions."

She smiled wanly. "You know, in the interest of Christmas, I'll even take a chance on your cooking tonight. What the heck.''

Joe turned on the oven and started to unwrap the plastic from the pizzas. ''I think you'll find your trust is well placed.'' Frozen cheese scattered on the countertop, and Joe paused before brushing it back onto the pizza. ''This would be difficult to ruin.'' He slipped an oven mitt onto his hand and lifted the pizza like a large flat baseball.

''Don't get cocky,'' she warned, watching him dust the frozen cheese and probably a few other miscellaneous crumbs onto their dinner. ''You don't want to put the pizzas in upside down, you know.''

He checked the frozen pizzas in the oven, then carefully turned one over so the cheese was on the top. When he turned back to Darcy he splayed his arms, spatula in one hand, oven mitt on the other. ''No problem.''

''Why is this blinking?'' Ricky asked. They looked and saw that he was sitting by the answering machine.

''Oh.'' When was the last time she'd checked the machine? She had the sudden, irrational hope that maybe the buyer was backing out of the deal. ''That means there's a message,'' Darcy said with a frown. ''I don't think I've checked it for a couple of days.'' She went over and pushed the play button with a trembling hand.

It was the realtor. Darcy's heart felt as if it stopped when she heard the familiar voice. According to the machine, she'd called for two days running and left three messages. ''I just wanted to let you know before we went to settlement that you've had another offer. It seems one of your neighbors, a Mr.—'' paper rustled in the background ''—Keller, Lyndon Keller, is very eager to buy the five-hundred acres to the west. Of course I told him it was out of the question—that you were signing a contract on Tuesday. But he insisted I ask and that I tell you he'll grant the easement you've requested on the other side of the property.'' She went on to give the figure he'd offered:

three times Darcy and Joe's investment in the property so far.

The second and third messages from the realtor were much the same, and she left her office, home, and beeper numbers, with instructions for them to call as soon as they got the message.

Darcy looked at Joe. "What do you make of that?" Her voice shook. Please don't let him blow it off, please, she prayed silently. Give us a chance to make this work.

His face had grown pale. "I'm not sure what to make of it." He cleared his throat. "You, ah, you do realize what this means."

She nodded slowly. "That we—at least I—could stay, and we would still have enough profit that we could both repay our debts." Or you could take me with you, she thought madly. I don't want to go back to the city at all, but I especially don't want to go back without you.

A brief picture of him in the city with her flew to mind and she acknowledged he could never be happy there. And neither could she, she realized now.

Darcy saw Joe glance at Ricky. Understanding the importance of keeping this conversation between the adults, she hesitated. Fortunately the child had gone back to the toy train and was in his own little world. "But maybe you should. If you can, I mean. Ricky doesn't seem to want to go."

"Do *you* want to go?" Joe asked her, blue eyes for once questioning instead of holding their usual sharp confidence.

"Well...what do *you* want to do?" she returned, afraid to give herself away.

"I'm not sure." He eyed her carefully, set the spatula down and pulled the oven mitt off. There was a pad of paper on the end of the kitchen counter; he picked it up on his way past. "So let's make a list of our options."

"Okay." She went over to the couch and sat on the end,

facing him. The lights from the tree winked in the corner of her eye, but her attention was focused tremulously on Joe.

"We'll have one column for keeping the ranch and one for selling." He drew lines on the paper. "So. Reasons to go. First, there's profit."

"Big profit," she agreed.

"Huge." He drew a money sign. "Bigger than either of us had a right to hope for."

"Absolutely."

"Okay." He put another money sign down. "Profit. Next..." He thought for a moment, tapping the pen against his chin.

"Opportunity," Darcy said. "It sounds like your sister-in-law has a huge operation going out there in Oklahoma. It's a great opportunity to be the foreman of an important ranch."

Joe shrugged, then nodded and jotted something down. "It's an opportunity of a sort. Of course, it's an opportunity to make someone else's place successful, not my own." He jotted again, this time on the other side of the paper. "So those two really sort of cancel each other out."

"I guess they do." Darcy nodded again.

"But there's opportunity for *you*," he pointed out. "You get to go to the big city on the west coast and do that scholarship work."

"Actually, I'm thinking maybe I'll find a place quieter than the city. I've gotten used to being a hermit."

"What about your work?"

She shrugged. "With computers and the Internet, I can do that work from anywhere. Maybe...maybe I'll move to a little place in the country."

"That's really what you want to do?"

She hesitated for only a moment. "Yeah."

He started to write, but she stopped him.

"Wait," she said. "Which column are you putting that in?"

He looked at her in surprise. "The Reasons to Sell column." He didn't say "of course," but it was written all over his face.

"Put it in the other column," she told him.

"What?"

"Really. I've probably gotten a little backwards being here for so long, but the big city life doesn't hold the same appeal that it once did." She waved her hand. "Put it in the Reasons Not to Sell column."

"You're sure?"

"Yes," she said evenly, trying to hold his gaze with her own, trying to say a million things with her eyes that she couldn't say with her voice. "I'm sure."

"All right, then." She saw his smile as he looked down at the paper. "What else should we put in the Reasons to Sell column?"

"Hmm." There was a moment of silence as they both mulled it over. "You put profit down?"

He tapped the pen on the pad. "First thing."

There was another long moment of silence. The music had stopped but the hum of the toy train ran in the background, punctuated by the occasional crackle of the fire.

"Let's switch to the other column for a minute, then. Reasons to stay." She snuck a furtive glance at Joe. "Hmm...let's see."

"Your family heritage," Joe said triumphantly. "You could keep the place in your family for a little longer."

"True. And you would have your own place to make something of, instead of someone else's."

"That's right." He scribbled on the paper.

"We've hired some men," Darcy added. "We'd be able to keep them on instead of unemploying them right after Christmas. That's a horrible time to be without a job. Especially when you have a family."

"Good one." He wrote it down.

"You know," Darcy said slowly, measuring her words, "it sounds like we'd *both* be staying on if we didn't sell. As I recall, that wasn't a prospect that appealed to you very much in the beginning."

"I believe *you* were the one who reacted with open-mouthed horror at the idea."

"I did not."

"You did. I remember it clearly."

So do I, she thought. "Well, it hasn't been as bad as I thought it would be."

He looked at her and his mouth curled into a slow smile. "You're not saying you like it, are you?"

Her face grew hot, but she smiled, too. "I haven't *hated* it." She looked at the paper and tried to change the subject. "What else should we put on that side?"

"There is one more thing." His voice was almost shy, which was totally uncharacteristic.

Her breath caught in her throat. "What's that?"

His eyes flicked down to the page and he muttered something that she couldn't understand but that she could have sworn contained the words "I love you."

"What did you say?"

He looked at her, a little shocked by her response. "You're right. Scratch that." He drew a line through something on the paper.

"No, I didn't hear you. I didn't hear what you said." It was taking a chance, but she had to find out. "What did you say?"

"I said—" he cleared his throat and his face grew unmistakably flushed "—that I love you." He gave a shake of his head. "And if you stayed, we could get married and raise a family here." He met her eyes and there was an apologetic smile in his. "Which is probably a stupid idea."

Darcy threw her arms around his neck and squeezed tight. "You're probably right, it probably *is* a stupid idea."

She kissed his face, his chin, his hair, his ear. For the first time in years she felt ecstatic. "But I love you, too."

He clasped his arms around her back. "So you're willing to give this a try?"

Tears filled her eyes and spilled out over her cheeks. "I am if you are. In fact, I am even if you're not!"

"You're not just being swept away by the romance of the meal, are you?"

She laughed. "No, I'm not. I've been so afraid to...to say anything to you because I thought you weren't...you didn't feel the same way..."

He took her hands in his. "Then I should do this right, shouldn't I?" He got down on his knees before her. "Darcy Beckett, you are the most beautiful, loving, intelligent woman I have ever known, and I love you more than anything else on this earth. Would you...please...do me the honor of becoming my wife?"

A sob caught in her throat. "Yes," she whispered. "Oh, yes, Joe. I will."

"I love you, Darcy," he said. "I always have."

"I love you, too," she returned, finally allowing herself to feel all of the things she had wanted to feel for so long. "And I always will."

"What's going on?" Ricky asked from behind them.

They flew apart and turned to face him, Darcy swiping the tears off her cheeks.

Ricky looked at her, alarmed. "What's wrong?"

"Absolutely nothing." She beamed at him. "We have some wonderful news for you."

"You do?" He looked from her to Joe.

Joe nodded. "We're staying." He put his arm around Darcy and pulled her closer. "Darcy and I are going to get married and this is going to be our home, so..." He could hear a quaver in his own voice, and he paused before finishing, "So the whole family is staying home."

"Forever?" Ricky asked.

Joe and Darcy looked at each other, then both said, simultaneously, "Forever."

"But I thought you had to kiss more."

Joe glanced at Darcy. "We will."

"And hug more."

Darcy smiled. "Definitely."

Ricky wrinkled his nose. "Is there anything else?"

Darcy laughed, and Joe said, "I'm sure we'll think of something."

*   *   *   *   *

Take 2 bestselling love stories FREE

Plus get a FREE surprise gift!

Special Limited-Time Offer

Mail to Silhouette Reader Service™

3010 Walden Avenue
P.O. Box 1867
Buffalo, N.Y. 14240-1867

YES! Please send me 2 free Silhouette Romance™ novels and my free surprise gift. Then send me 6 brand-new novels every month, which I will receive months before they appear in bookstores. Bill me at the low price of $2.90 each plus 25¢ delivery and applicable sales tax, if any.* That's the complete price, and a saving of over 10% off the cover prices—quite a bargain! I understand that accepting the books and gift places me under no obligation ever to buy any books. I can always return a shipment and cancel at any time. Even if I never buy another book from Silhouette, the 2 free books and the surprise gift are mine to keep forever.

215 SEN CH7S

Name	(PLEASE PRINT)	
Address		Apt. No.
City	State	Zip

This offer is limited to one order per household and not valid to present Silhouette Romance™ subscribers. *Terms and prices are subject to change without notice. Sales tax applicable in N.Y.

USROM-98

©1990 Harlequin Enterprises Limited

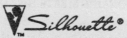

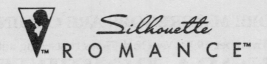

COMING NEXT MONTH